She had just enough willpower to pull away.

But as she moved, Nick muttered, "No," and his mouth came down again, coaxing hers open in a kiss so deep and intimate that it leached the strength from her bones.

The aroused hunger of his body transmitted its own particular spell. Minerva's arms slid around his shoulders; slow and seductive as a cat, she arched against him, inciting him with small, barely perceptible movements of her body, whipping up an appetite that had been smoldering for too long.

ROBYN DONALD has always lived in Northland in New Zealand, initially on her father's stud dairy farm at Warkworth, then in the Bay of Islands, an area of great natural beauty where she lives today with her husband and one corgi dog. She resigned her teaching position when she found she enjoyed writing romances more, and now spends any time not writing in reading, gardening, traveling and writing letters to keep up with her two adult children and her friends.

Books by Robyn Donald

Don't miss any of our special offers. Write to us at the following address for information on our newest releases.

Harlequin Reader Service
U.S.: 3010 Walden Ave., P.O. Box 1325, Buffalo, NY 14269
Canadian: P.O. Box 609, Fort Erie, Ont. L2A 5X3

ROBYN DONALD

The Colour of Midnight

Harlequin Books

TORONTO • NEW YORK • LONDON
AMSTERDAM • PARIS • SYDNEY • HAMBURG
STOCKHOLM • ATHENS • TOKYO • MILAN
MADRID • WARSAW • BUDAPEST • AUCKLAND

For my mother, Iris Leabourn Hutching, who, forced by circumstances to give up some of her dreams, made sure that each of her six children got the chance to follow theirs. She kept her sense of humor and compassion intact through it all, and is the best cook in New Zealand, which is only one of the reasons her children love her.

ISBN 0-373-11714-0

THE COLOUR OF MIDNIGHT

Copyright © 1994 by Robyn Donald.

CHAPTER ONE

'THERE should,' Minerva Robertson muttered as she peered through the rain, 'be signs on that signpost, damn it. Wretched vandals.'

Her voice, oddly deep for such a slight person, was tinged by a British accent, the inevitable outcome of two years spent as the cook on a yacht owned by a British billionaire and crewed by British sailors. Now back in New Zealand, she was working hard to get rid of it.

Unless she could work out which road she should take, she was going to have to go back. Somewhere, not too far away, was a huge sheep and cattle station called Spanish Castle. The place might, she thought with an irritation that was tinged with foreboding, as well be in Spain.

For the last five days she had slowly meandered north from Auckland, telling herself she was on holiday. At a loose end when her father and stepmother had left for a business trip to North America, she'd decided to see a little of New Zealand's long northern peninsula. Even as close as Kerikeri, twenty kilometres or so away, she had had no intention of visiting the place where her stepsister had spent the last year of her life.

Until she'd seen the signpost. Spanish Castle, it had said, and pointed inland.

Without really making a conscious decision Minerva had followed that imperative finger.

Not, she thought now, switching warm air up on to the windscreen in an effort to clean the thick film of condensation from it, one of my better ideas.

Both roads looked equally dismal; both seemed to dwindle into pot-holed tracks beneath the huge, primeval presence of the *kauri* forest. If she hadn't seen that signpost at the bottom of the hill she'd be wondering whether she'd taken a wrong turning somewhere.

As it was, she had to say out loud, 'You know you're on the right road, idiot. Spanish Castle is somewhere up here, down one of these hopeless-looking roads. And the weather is pure coincidence—in New Zealand it always rains in the spring!'

Muttering, she opened an umbrella and dashed through the merciless rain, skidding to a halt in the tangle of long, exceedingly wet grass that surrounded the base of the signpost. A few mustard-coloured splinters lurking coyly in the mud put paid to her idea of fitting the smashed signs to the jagged stumps and working out which road led where.

Gloomily, she turned back towards the car.

And gasped.

Unheard above the persistent drumming of raindrops on the umbrella, a man had solidified from the mist and the murk. Clad in a riding coat, he was on the back of a large grey horse; a black and white sheepdog lay in front of him over the shoulders of the horse. All three, dog, man, horse, were regarding her with an aloof surprise that wasn't mitigated in the least by the slow, almost involuntary wag of the dog's tail.

Minerva essayed a tentative smile, trying to forget that she hadn't seen a house for the last three miles, and that around them were several thousand hectares of bush, sombre and dank and almost pathless.

As though on cue the rain eased off, then miraculously stopped. All she could hear was the distant rush of some stream and the faint drip of diverted raindrops in the bush.

'Don't wave that umbrella around,' the man said curtly, the lean hand holding the reins moving slightly as the horse danced sideways. Almost immediately the animal subsided into stillness again, although it eyed her with the same wary caution as the man and the dog.

Even with rain trickling down the austere angles of his face, the rider emanated a controlled power and strength that was very intimidating.

Minerva's hand clenched on the handle of the umbrella. 'I'm sorry,' she said gruffly, hoping that her nervousness didn't show in her tone. 'Can you tell me which road leads to Spanish Castle?'

He surveyed her with unnervingly pale eyes that looked through her rather than at her, although she was prepared to bet that nothing escaped his notice. He reminded her, she thought foolishly, of some grim conquistador viewing yet another country to be plundered, without passion, without even a rage for riches, to be looted and sacked simply because it was there.

The horse moved restlessly, flicking its ears. A shiver tightened Minerva's skin. The man and his mount were taking on an almost mythic quality, remote, clothed in darkly shimmering veils of fantasy and legend. Even the dog, unnaturally sapient, looked like a being from another world!

'It's a cattle station around here somewhere,' she said politely, striving to regain her normal pragmatic outlook. 'It belongs to a Mr Peveril. Nick Peveril.'

'I know who it belongs to.' The even, darkly textured voice was toneless. 'Why do you want to go there?'

Minerva's indigo eyes glittered as her chin came up. 'Is that any business of yours?'

He inclined his head, his gaze never leaving her heart-shaped face. 'I think so. I own Spanish Castle.'

She should have known. She'd seen photographs, but the groom who had smiled back from the prints had looked completely different from this man. Of course, they were wedding photos. Everyone always looked happy in wedding photos.

'Mr Peveril,' she said, looking, she hoped, confident and in control, 'I'm Minerva Robertson.'

His brows drew together. 'Are you?' he said without the slightest flicker of interest. 'Am I expecting you?'

Something shrivelled inside her. 'I'm Stella's sister,' she told him crisply.

The hand on the reins jerked; as the horse moved uneasily the dog turned its head and looked a moment up into the lean, harsh-featured face.

'I see,' Nick Peveril said.

How could Stella have married this cold fish?

Minerva said brightly, 'I'm home from abroad and I decided to come north for a holiday, because Ruth and Dad are away.'

Ruth had mentioned Nick Peveril in passing, but how close they were Minerva didn't know. He certainly wasn't giving any clues; that hard, expressionless face didn't alter as he nodded. She ploughed on with a touch of defiance, 'I didn't really intend to come here, but I saw the sign at the bottom of the hill so—well, here I am.'

The sound of her babbling disconcerted her so much that she stopped and took a horrified breath. Damn it, she wasn't going to lose her composure just because Stella's husband looked at her as though she was something revolting and slimy he'd found under a stone.

'I'm sorry I was less than welcoming,' he said, still in that level tone that revealed nothing. A whip-flick of cynicism robbed his smile of humour. 'I had no idea you were back.'

'I've been home for three weeks.'

He nodded, his eyes not leaving her face. 'Spanish Castle's only a couple of miles down the road to the left. You'll see the gateposts. Left again inside, and follow the drive to the homestead. When you get there, tell Mrs Borrows who you are. Are you staying?'

'No,' she said too quickly. 'I'm going to spend the night in Mangonui at the backpackers' hostel there.'

He didn't look relieved. He didn't, she thought with a waspishness that surprised her, look anything except austere and impervious and infinitely remote.

'I hope it's not too inconvenient,' she said sweetly, essaying a smile.

It didn't evoke any response. Minerva was suddenly conscious that she wore no make-up at all and that her long ash-brown hair was probably hanging in strings down her back, dulled by the rain into an undistinguished mouse colour.

'Not in the least. I'll be there as soon as I can.' An imperceptible signal propelled the big horse across the road and through a gate she hadn't noticed. The horse turned; with a skill indicative of long practice, and a brutal economy of movement unhindered by the heavy riding coat, Stella's widower bent and pushed the gate closed. Straightening, he lifted a hand in what might have been a mocking salute, then urged the horse forward again.

The mist swallowed them up, horse, dog and man, as though they had never existed.

Minerva stared stupidly after them until her stiff hands and wet feet recalled her to herself. So that was Nick Peveril! She shivered. He was—elemental, a fit denizen for this gloomy, rain-soaked landscape. Yet Stella had written glowingly of his laughter, his kindness and his fascinating sophistication.

There was nothing amusing, kind or sophisticated about this man. He was made of much more primal stuff. In spite of that pale horse, he looked like the dark lord of Hades himself. However, there was no need to surrender to the chill that crawled down her spine. She was no virginal Persephone, to be snapped up as a pretty trophy to brighten his gloomy kingdom.

It was Stella he had swept away in a whirlwind courtship that had lasted a bare month. In spite of her ravishing beauty and her affairs Stella had been oddly inexperienced and Nick Peveril was the first man she had ever loved.

Yet he had killed her as surely as if it had been one of those lean strong hands that had measured out the infamous combination of sedatives and tranquillisers and painkillers that had put an end to her twenty-six years of life.

Minerva wriggled back into the car, held the umbrella out of the door and shook it vigorously before thrusting it on to a plastic bag in the back. Turning around, she slammed the door shut and gripped the wheel, gazing ahead with eyes that stung.

Only then did she admit that the real reason she had taken the road to Spanish Castle was that she wanted to know what had gone wrong with her sister's idyll.

Although almost a year had passed since Stella's death, Minerva had come back to a house that still mourned. Oh, Ruth, Stella's mother, smiled a lot, but her strenuously bright manner didn't hide the fact that she was too thin, her carefully coiffed hair grey, her pretty face haggard. Minerva had been shocked and alarmed.

That night she had sat talking with her father long after Ruth had gone to bed, finally saying bluntly, 'She hasn't got over it, has she?'

'No.' Her father set down his glass of whisky; it was almost water, as it had been ever since Minerva was old enough to remember. A prosperous businessman, Brian Robertson was abstemious by nature. He'd used to tease Ruth by telling her he'd married her to provide a bit of drama to his boringly normal life. It didn't look as though he had teased his wife for a long time.

Now he said heavily, 'I don't think she'll ever get over it. She still cries every night.' His mouth tightened. 'She waits until she thinks I'm asleep and then she weeps into her pillow. It rips me to pieces. She feels so guilty, as though she failed Stella, and I can't get her to understand that Stella was a grown woman, old enough to be responsible for her actions. Ruth thinks she should have seen what was happening.'

Minerva rubbed at the frown between her brows. 'Poor Ruth.'

'I'm worried,' Brian said unnecessarily. 'She's slipping away from me. If only she knew why Stella killed herself!'

'Nothing's turned up? No other letter?' She knew the answer, but she asked just the same.

'No.' Brian sipped his drink, his pleasant, good-looking face set in lines it hadn't had a year before. 'Just the note she left for Nick, and that told us nothing.'

Both were silent. 'I'm so sorry', Stella had scrawled with an unusual economy of words. 'Please try to forgive me'.

'What about Nick? He must have some inkling of what went wrong.'

'He's just as much in the dark as we are. It shattered him.'

'He must know *something*.'

But her father shook his head. 'He says he doesn't, and I believe him.'

Her father was an acute judge of men, but now, as Minerva switched on the engine, she wondered. The man who had appeared out of the mist didn't look as though he would balk at lying if it suited him. Had he lied about his wife's state of mind?

Setting a jaw that gave definition and character to her rather indeterminate features, Minerva put the car in gear and drove carefully through the thinning mist.

Just inside the gates she stopped, looking to the right at the great pile of rock which a hundred years ago had given the first Nicholas Peveril the name for his land. The eroded neck of an ancient volcano, it reared high above the surrounding countryside. Cloud drifted low across the sheer rock faces, moving on invisible winds, parting to reveal trees clinging to clefts and fissures in the cliffs. Dramatic and awe-inspiring, it did look like the massive ruins of some gaunt castle of the giants.

A shiver of apprehension pulled the tiny hairs of Minerva's skin upright.

'Stop being so jittery and stupid,' she told herself as she put the car in motion again. 'You've seen Igor, and he wasn't so bad. No obvious fangs, and a horse and a dog instead of bats!'

Nick Peveril was clearly a good farmer. The fences were in excellent repair, as were the various buildings, and the grass in the paddocks lay thick and lush in its spring growth.

He was also a good employer. The farm workers' cottages were big, well-cared-for, and set in substantial gardens.

But the homestead was breathtaking, a huge double-storeyed building that must have been built by that first Nicholas, for it was a Victorian structure of weather-boards, with more than a hint of the severe, satisfying proportions of the Georgian style it had supplanted.

Shading the front veranda was a wistaria vine that was probably as old as the house. Its thick stems were hazed by bronzed, gleaming new growth, punctuated by fat buds silver in the rain.

A wide flight of wooden steps led up to the veranda. On either side of a glass-panelled front door French windows with panes of glass above stretched in ordered pairs down the side of the house. This was one nine-teenth-century villa that wouldn't be dark inside.

And the garden was like something out of a fairy-tale, a bower of skilfully contrasted form and colour, each glowing flower, each leaf, sprinkled by crystals of rain.

Minerva switched off the engine and got out. From somewhere around the back of the house a dog barked, warning the inhabitants that a stranger was near. Heavy, unsettling scent from the roses mingled with the rich perfume of a white rhododendron beside the steps. More roses, miniatures planted in clay pots, ascended on either side of the steps; as she moved between them perfume billowed into the moist air, adding to the mingled scents that drifted from the plants in the wide bed beneath the veranda.

Minerva's nerves tingled. Holding herself very erect, smiling sardonically because it was ridiculous to imagine that the place was welcoming her, she walked to the door.

Before she had time to ring the bell or use the knocker the door opened. A middle-aged woman with a harassed expression looked enquiringly at her.

'I'm Minerva Robertson,' Minerva said, smiling. 'Mrs Peveril's sister.'

'Mrs Pev—— Oh!' For a shocking moment the woman looked appalled.

'I met Mr Peveril along the road,' Minerva said smoothly, struggling to hide a fierce, corroding anger. 'I've just called in. I'm on my way north.'

'Oh. Yes, of course. Do come in.' Collecting herself with an obvious effort, Mrs Borrows held the door open.

Minerva, who had some experience of old wooden houses, braced herself as she walked into a wide hall decorated in paper the rich gold of Jersey cream. But instead of the damp rawness she expected, the place was warm and dry.

The temperature was a definite bonus. It wasn't a centrally heated stuffiness, more a gentle, all-pervading warmth that banished the bone-chilling dankness Minerva had experienced in other old houses.

Over the years she'd worked in the kitchens of several very expensively decorated houses. Some she had liked, some she had found soulless. The homestead at Spanish Castle had been decorated by someone with great skill and a definite empathy for Victorian architecture. Minerva's gaze skimmed a splendid console table on a mellow Persian runner. Reflected in the gilt-framed Regency mirror above was a bunch of apricot and yellow and white old-fashioned roses in a silver vase, their sweetness almost unbearably evocative.

Beyond the table an elegant staircase ascended to the first floor. Gilt-framed pictures, mostly of an age in keeping with the house, were displayed carefully, and there were flowers everywhere.

'This is beautiful,' she said softly, looking around her with pleasure. 'How old is it?'

'A hundred and twenty years.

'It doesn't show its age.'

'Spanish Castle has always been well-cared-for,' the housekeeper said as though she'd been accused of neglecting her duty. 'Would you like to come in here?'

She led Minerva into a small formal parlour decorated in the same sunny shades, although here the colours were less intense as befitted a room where people spent time rather than passed through.

'Would you like a cup of tea while you're waiting for Mr Peveril?' Mrs Borrows asked punctiliously.

Minerva was already regretting her impulsive decision to drive up that long road from Kerikeri. The house might be welcoming but its inhabitants certainly weren't. Still, she was here now; she'd have a cup of tea, exchange a few words with Nick Peveril, and then leave.

'Yes, thank you.' Her throaty voice was just as impersonally polite as the older woman's.

She didn't look around until the older woman had left. The little room could have been too stiff with its delicately formal seats and desk, but the pieces of furniture had the air of having lived so long together that they had settled into an amiable, comfortable companionship.

Outside the French windows an emerald lawn swept to a wide band of sheltering trees thickly planted at the base with rhododendrons and daphne, pieris and more roses. Minerva's eyes lingered on one particularly glorious golden one until it was blotted out by a thick curtain of rain, heavy and implacable.

She turned away.

Almost immediately the housekeeper returned with a tray; she had barely set it down when her employer walked in, instantly dominating the small, decorous room.

It was the unexpectedness of his arrival that took Minerva's breath away, nothing else. She hadn't expected him so soon; he must have taken a short-cut. When her heart had slowed down a bit she realised that he probably wasn't much taller than her father, only a couple of inches over six feet. But that air of cool authority, allied to the cool, inimical survey of his strange colourless eyes, made her feel small and defenceless.

'Hello,' she said, producing a polite smile.

'So you found your way here.' He was amazingly handsome, in a remote, arrogantly patrician manner. 'Welcome to Spanish Castle. Helen, could I have a cup, too?'

'I've put one there for you,' the housekeeper said.

He looked at her. 'Any call yet?'

'No.' The housekeeper looked excited and worried at the same time.

'Let me know when it comes through,' he said.

Smiling, she replied, 'Yes, of course.'

No formality *there*, Minerva thought as the older woman left the room.

'Would you like to pour? Mrs Borrows's daughter is in labour in Christchurch,' Nick Peveril explained. 'It's the first grandchild, so she's very excited. How did you enjoy sailing the world on your billionaire's yacht?'

'He wasn't *my* billionaire,' Minerva said lightly, smiling with more than a little irony at the memory of the portly, harried man who'd spent no more than three weeks playing in his expensive state-of-the-art toy during the two years she had sailed on it. 'I was merely the cook. I enjoyed it very much. Do you take milk?'

'Thank you. No sugar.'

As he took the cup and saucer from her she noted his beautiful hands, strong with long, callused fingers, tanned like his face almost to copper. The sight of those hands dealing efficiently with the elegant china cup made something contract suddenly in Minerva's stomach.

'It seems an unusual career for a woman with all your advantages.'

At least he accepted that it was a career! Minerva gave the usual smile and the usual answer. 'It's my one talent, and I enjoy doing it.'

'You don't stay in any job for very long. Stella said that the longest you lasted was usually a year.'

'I'm not into the old-retainer bit, so I sign short contracts,' she said steadily, resenting his comment even though there hadn't been a hint of censure in the deep voice. 'That way I get to see the world and experience it a bit more intimately than a tourist does.'

'You must really have enjoyed it to spend two years on the yacht.'

She had just joined the crew when Stella wrote to tell her she was getting married. Because of a glitch in the postal arrangements the letter hadn't caught up with her until a month after the wedding. It hadn't seemed worthwhile to come back then.

And she had been in the middle of the Atlantic, bucketing through a hurricane, when Stella suffered her lonely death. As soon as they reached land she had flown back, arriving too late for the funeral, but able to mourn with Ruth and her father and her half-brother Kane for a couple of weeks before flying back.

Minerva nodded. 'The billionaire insisted on two-year contracts, and I wanted the job enough to make an exception for him.'

'The great New Zealand overseas experience.' He had a beautiful voice, rich and many-layered, but it had remarkably little expression: as little as his face, or the silver-grey eyes. They should have been translucent, but the polished metallic sheen successfully hid any emotion.

This withdrawn, reserved man had retired behind the formidable barricades of his self-sufficiency. Unease slithered the length of her spine, gathered in an unpleasant pool at the pit of her stomach.

'I suppose it has to do with living on three small islands at the bottom of the map,' she returned conversationally. 'To get anywhere at all you have to fly for hours, so why not go the whole hog and see the rest of the world while you're about it?'

His smile was cynical. 'And broaden your insular mind.'

She lifted thin eyebrows. 'Some people merely hone their prejudices.'

'That's astute of you.'

'I suppose you've done a fair amount of travelling,' she said, unable to decide whether he was being sarcastic or not.

'Yes. But my most vivid memories are of the first time I was on my own. I came overland from India and hitchhiked around Europe, spent six months in England, then went on one of those truck tours through Africa to Cape Town, before coming back across Canada and America.'

In any other man she would have thought she heard wistfulness in his tone, but it was impossible to think of this man as being wistful. He exuded a self-confidence so imposing and uncompromising that she was more than a little threatened by it.

'Sounds fun,' she said neutrally. He had changed from his farm clothes into a pair of well-tailored trousers and a fine cotton shirt. Few men in New Zealand had their shirts made for them, but Minerva was positive that this one had been cut especially to fit his broad shoulders and muscular arms.

It was difficult to imagine the man who lived in this house and wore those clothes backpacking around the world. She flicked a swift glance at his face. The angular features and straight mouth spoke of strength and uncompromising purpose. No matter how hard she tried she couldn't envisage him as a carefree youth.

Her gaze dropped to her teacup as she was undermined by a sense of dislocation, a shifting of the foundations. Nick Peveril, with his impassive face and deliberate, guarded composure, bore no resemblance at all to the man of whom Stella had written so ecstatically.

When he spoke again Minerva's cup rattled in its saucer. Watch what you're doing, she scolded herself, setting it down on the table by her chair.

'How long are you home for?' he asked.

'A month.' A substantial bonus meant she could afford a lazy summer, but her plans for the future were going to need money, so it would join the rest of her savings.

'And then what? Stella seemed to think that you intended to settle permanently here sooner or later.'

She shrugged. 'One of these days I'm going to come back and open my own restaurant, but for the moment I like my life. I've been offered a job in the British Virgin Islands with an expatriate family.'

When he smiled one corner of his mouth lifted higher than the other. 'You'll be able to work on your tan,' he said lightly. Something flickered in the frosty brilliance of his eyes.

It made her distinctly uneasy. In a voice that could have starched a dozen tablecloths, she said, 'The hole in the ozone layer has put an end to roasting in the sun, but I'm looking forward to it. I believe it's extraordinarily beautiful there.' Before she had time to wonder whether it was sensible, she added, 'Stella and I used to promise each other that one day we'd go to the Caribbean and drink rum and play in a steel band.'

'She wouldn't have liked it, unless you stayed in a luxury hotel. For some strange reason I expected you to look like her,' he said, pale eyes opaque. 'Stupid, I know. You don't share even a parent in common, do you?'

'No, we're a blended family. Stella and I were no relation at all, really, which is why she was beautiful and I'm not.'

The minute she said it she knew it was a mistake. It sounded like a cheap appeal for compliments. She opened her mouth to qualify the statement, then closed it firmly.

'Yes, she was,' he said. 'But you're very attractive too, as I'm sure you know.'

He wasn't so crass as to look her over, but an undertone in the enigmatic voice made her aware that he had noticed the long, coltish legs in her jeans, the gentle curves of her breasts, and the indentation of her narrow waist.

A kind of outrage, mingled with a suspicious warmth, sent colour scudding through her white skin. Not for the first time she wished she had Stella's even tan. For her stepsister a blush had merely been a slight deepening of the apricot skin over her cheekbones; for Minerva it was an embarrassing betrayal.

She strove for objectivity. Men did notice women—it was a simple fact of life. They enjoyed with their eyes. Women did, too.

After all, she had observed that because his mouth was intriguingly lop-sided each rare smile hinted of wryness. She'd registered the thick black lashes and dark brows surrounding those amazingly limpid, guarded eyes, and now that his hair was drying she'd realised it was the colour of manuka honey, a warm, rich amber with golden highlights set there by the northern sun.

She was unreservedly grateful when Mrs Borrows came too quickly in through the door, her face unnaturally disciplined. 'Nick—oh, Nick! Murray's just rung,' she said without preamble, her voice breaking on the last word. 'Things are not going right. He—he thinks I should come down. As s-soon as I can.'

With the smooth speed Minerva had noticed before Nick got to his feet and went across to the housekeeper, sliding an unselfconscious arm around her shoulders, holding her while she fought for control.

'Pack your bag,' he ordered, 'and I'll get you to the airport in time to catch the afternoon plane to Auckland. I'll organise a flight through to Christchurch.'

'I can't go,' she said in muffled tones into his chest.

'Why not?'

'The dinner party you're giving on Saturday night for those Brazilians. This isn't Auckland, Nick, you can't just get in caterers, and there's no one here who could help you out with the cooking. Jillian's not——'

'Well, that's where you're wrong. Providentially, Minerva is a professional cook,' he said calmly, silver eyes lancing across to where Minerva sat, frozen with dismay as she realised the implications. 'She'll be more than happy to stay and see to it that our South American guests are fed. Won't you, Minerva?' It was no question. The icy transparency of his gaze had hardened into a silent command.

Minerva's brain closed down. She didn't want to stay here! But of course she nodded. And when she saw Mrs Borrows lift her head to look at her with dawning hope she knew she couldn't have refused.

'Yes, I can do it,' she said.

'Are you sure?' The housekeeper was obviously trying hard to be convinced.

Minerva nodded. 'Tell me what you've organised and I guarantee I'll have it on the table at the right time and cooked properly,' she promised, her tone revealing such complete confidence that Mrs Borrows relaxed.

Yet she still hesitated. 'It doesn't seem right,' she said, looking from Minerva's face to Nick's.

He said calmly, 'Helen, Minerva is family.'

Minerva smiled. 'That's what families are for,' she supplied. 'Coming to the rescue. Don't worry about it, I'll be glad to help out.'

This was the right note to take. Her voice quivering, the housekeeper said, 'Oh, thank you. I'll get a bag packed,' and hurried from the room.

Half an hour later they were seated in a large green Range Rover, travelling at a fair pace down the road Minerva had inched up so short a time before. Mrs Borrows was giving Minerva instructions, instructions Minerva didn't need. However, she sat through them, asking questions when it seemed the older woman had run out. For the next two and a half hours until the housekeeper got to Christchurch she'd have nothing to do but worry; Minerva's questions at least kept her mind occupied now.

Although the rain had eased again, the road was still slippery enough for the Range Rover to skid. That it didn't was due to the skill of the man driving. Minerva, inclined to be a nervous passenger with a driver she didn't know, soon gave up keeping her eye on the road ahead. Nick Peveril knew what he was doing.

They were ten minutes late, but the plane waited. Probably even large jumbo jets would wait for this man.

After a hasty goodbye Mrs Borrows ran across to the little aircraft and the door was swung shut behind her.

'Hello, Nick,' a laughing feminine voice said from behind. 'The baby arrived, has it?'

He turned. 'On its way,' he said, that powerfully attractive smile crinkling the corners of his eyes.

The woman was one Genevieve Chatswood, thirtyish, smart in jeans and a Liberty print shirt with a navy woollen jersey over it, her slim feet in boots. As Nick made the introductions she eyed Minerva with cool but unmistakable interest.

'Oh. Stella's sister? You don't look much alike.'

'We were stepsisters,' Minerva explained, trying to hide the note of resignation in her voice. 'Her mother married my father.'

After a dismissive look Genevieve transferred her attention to the man beside her. Frowning, she asked, 'Nick, if Mrs Borrows has had to go, what are you doing for Saturday night?'

'Ah, that's where the light hand of serendipity comes in,' he said blandly. 'Minerva will deal with it all. She's a professional chef.'

'How—fortunate,' Genevieve said, her voice cooling rapidly. 'Do you plan to stay long, Minerva?'

'No.' Minerva left it at that. She wasn't going to answer questions from someone who had no right to ask them.

Nick said evenly, 'Minerva is on holiday in the north. I hope to persuade her to stay on for a few days after the dinner.' His enigmatic gaze rested a moment on Minerva's shuttered face.

Genevieve's green eyes narrowed a second, then opened wide. She flashed a smile at Nick. 'Well, if you need any help, let me know, won't you? I'd be quite happy to act as hostess for you again.' The dazzling smile dimmed noticeably when it was transferred to Minerva. 'I'd better go. I've just put ten boxes of orchids on the plane for Auckland; I've got to pick another fifty boxes to catch the flight to Japan tomorrow. See you Saturday!'

She strode away, confident, sure of her attraction and her competence. Minerva watched her departure thoughtfully. Genevieve Chatswood had lost no time in staking her claim. If that was the sort of woman Kerikeri bred, it was no wonder Stella had found it difficult to make friends.

Since knowing Stella she had learned to feel sorry for beautiful people. They never knew whether they were admired for their looks or for themselves.

Not that the man who walked with an easy, effortless gait around the front of the Range Rover seemed to suffer any such problems. Resenting quite irrationally that air of complete and invincible confidence, Minerva hid a cynical little smile as she fastened her seatbelt. Nick Peveril looked like a Regency buck, with all the type's fabled pride and hauteur and air of self-contained assurance, as well as the elegance and *savoir faire*.

Perhaps he was too—too intense, too shut in on himself to have stepped from the pages of a Georgette Heyer novel. He was certainly a complex man, not a hearty, extroverted son of the soil.

However, he chose his accoutrements to fit his place in society. The Range Rover was exactly the right vehicle for the seriously rich pastoral aristocrat, and Spanish Castle the right setting. It was a pity the horse wasn't black; it should rear all over the place, and be called

Satan, or Demon, or Devil, and only ever be rideable by the lord of the house, but in spite of that it had looked the part perfectly.

Of course, the dog should be an aristocrat—a wolf-hound, or some kind of hunting, shooting and fishing dog, instead of a black and white sheepdog. But it had added the right touch. You couldn't have everything.

And in spite of his glacial demeanour, Nick made her more aware of her femininity than any other man since Paul Penn had seduced her when she was nineteen.

Which had to signal danger. Minerva looked straight ahead as he got in and switched on the engine.

Five silent minutes later he remarked casually, 'You won't have to do any of the housework. Helen has help three days a week from the wife of one of the stockmen. Just concentrate on the cooking.'

'Oh, I'll probably be able to manage a few light duties,' she said, hiding the amusement in her tone with mildness.

He smiled. It was like the sun breaking through storm clouds. Lop-sided, slightly twisted it might be, but the fundamental detachment that seemed to be an integral part of his personality was temporarily in retreat when he smiled.

Her stomach clenched. When the armour he imposed over his emotions was breached he was gorgeous.

No wonder Stella had tumbled headlong into love with him. The thought sent a faint feeling of nausea through Minerva, as though by responding to that inscrutable, remote charm she had been disloyal to her stepsister.

Resting her head on the back of the seat, Minerva stared with unseeing, half-closed eyes at the rain-swept countryside, brooding yet again over Stella's actions, wondering sickly what had driven her to take her own life.

There had been no reason for her to be depressed. She had had everything to live for; a husband she adored, a future that was shiny and sweet with the promise of happiness. She had been popular and loved, with an infectious, sparkling gaiety that attracted as much attention as her sultry, exotic beauty.

It was impossible to imagine Stella saving pills, stealing them from her mother and the housekeeper, hoarding them away in some horrible kind of squirrel's cache until she had garnered enough to snuff out her life. She'd waited until Nick had gone away for three days, then swallowed them deliberately, carefully, until they were all gone. It was appalling, hideous, yet she had done it, and left them all bewildered.

The housekeeper had found her the next morning. That must have been Helen Borrows. No wonder she had looked so horrified when Minerva told her she was Mrs Peveril's sister.

'Suicide while the balance of her mind was disturbed' had been the verdict at the inquest. Like Ruth, Minerva found this impossible to credit.

Stella had been so bright, so buoyantly high-spirited, so carefree as she flitted through her life. Oh, there had been moods. Stella's glums, the family had called them, and joined in an unspoken conspiracy to jolly her out of them. But they had never been particularly intense.

At the inquest Mrs Borrows had said that she hadn't noticed any signs of depression in the new Mrs Peveril, except that she seemed to be homesick and unable to settle in Northland. She had assumed it was because she didn't like living in the country. Some people didn't.

True enough. Yet Stella had seemed so in love with Nick that she would have lived anywhere just to be with him.

Admittedly, Stella hadn't exactly had much staying power when it came to men. Had that swift, fierce, passion burned out so quickly?

No, her adoring, almost awed love for Nick had resounded through her letters. Yet something had gone wrong. The last communication Minerva had received had been written three months before her stepsister killed herself. By then her letters had become oddly remote, a mere record of events, as though Stella had been trying to hide her real feelings behind the words.

Minerva bit her lip. Meeting Nick, seeing Spanish Castle with her own eyes, had only added to the mystery.

CHAPTER TWO

IN SILENCE they finished the drive back to the homestead. Nick parked the Range Rover in a garage which formed one side of a courtyard at the rear of the house. More flowers and a bed of herbs filled the corners of the courtyard. Like the rest of Spanish Castle it was picture-perfect.

'There's room for your car next door,' he said, and took her through into a double garage, one side of which was taken up by a large Mercedes-Benz saloon.

He opened the roller doors and watched while she drove Ruth's small car-about-town into the space next to the aristocrat. Once out, she unlocked the boot.

Looking what he was, a man so sure of his position in the world that he had no need to prove himself, a man accustomed to command, he extended an imperative hand. Well, he was stronger than she. With a mental shrug, Minerva passed him the pack that had accompanied her around the globe; in his leanly elegant hands it seemed a battered, cheap thing.

'This used to be a jumble of rooms,' he said, leading her through a door into an airy passageway that looked on to the courtyard. 'It's now garages and offices and mud-room. This doorway leads into the house proper.'

Up three steps, another wide hall stretched in front of them. He opened a door halfway down. 'Here's the kitchen,' he said.

It was superb. Checking it out with an authoritative eye, Minerva saw that it had been newly renovated and set up for entertaining. Not just the occasional dinner party, either. The French range had enough capacity to feed a hundred, and there was a big old wood range too, crackling softly to itself and giving off a very pleasant

26

heat. Clearly she'd found the source of the unexpected warmth throughout the house.

'Do you think you can manage the stoves?' Nick asked.

'No problem,' Minerva said reassuringly, trying to project a brisk, businesslike manner.

Of course her hair chose that moment to slip from its knot at the back of her head and slither down her back. Nick's gaze followed its downward passage until it reached her waist. Beneath the thick fringe of his lashes his eyes gleamed suddenly, something in that hooded scrutiny setting Minerva's cheeks aflame.

Turning away, she caught the fine, flyaway mass in two hands and ruthlessly anchored it in a knot at the back of her head, forcing the combs into the slippery, silky strands.

So much for her effort to be composed and matter-of-fact!

'I've cooked on everything from a campfire to a hotel range,' she told him firmly, trying to regain ground.

'Of course.' The cool eyes scanned her flushed, averted face. His uneven smile held more than a hint of mockery. 'You don't look like my idea of a chef.'

'Because I haven't got a white hat on? I only wear one in hotel kitchens.' Retreating behind a mask of expertise, she asked crisply, 'What foods do you dislike?'

'None. I'll eat anything you put in front of me provided it isn't too sweet.' He glanced at the thin watch on his strong wrist. 'We'll talk about my tastes later, after I've shown you the rest of the house and your room.'

A large tabby cat strolled casually in through the door, looked around with the air of one at home, then headed straight for him.

'This is Penelope,' he said, bending down to scratch her in exactly the right place behind her ears. 'Her official job is to keep any mice down.'

Minerva liked cats. This one, with its ineffable air of sleek self-respect, gave the huge kitchen a friendly, comfortable air. Purring, Penelope displayed herself sinuously about Nick's ankles, then, when he stood up, leapt gracefully on to a stool and looked expectantly at Minerva.

She laughed softly. 'Wait until dinner,' she said. 'And if I ever see you on the bench—watch it.'

The cat gave her a disgusted stare, yawned ostentatiously and settled down to wash its ears.

'Don't you like cats?' Nick asked.

'Love them, but with a cat it's always wise to establish right at the beginning who's boss. Penelope and I will get on very well, don't worry.' She stroked the blunt head, asking, 'What's your dog's name? The one you were carrying on your horse?'

'Rusty.'

Minerva's brows shot up. 'That's funny. I'd have bet money on him being black and white, without a speck of brown.'

'And you'd have won. I didn't name him,' he said, that half-smile softening his features.

'Who did?'

'The man who bred him. I've always assumed he was colourblind.'

'Does he come inside?' she asked. 'Rusty, I mean.'

His eyebrows lifted. 'No, he's a farm dog.'

So farm dogs were not pets. You learn something new every day, she told herself.

'I used to have a Labrador who did come inside,' he said, 'but Stella didn't like dogs, so when he died I didn't get another.'

There was a chilling lack of emotion in his tone, in his face, when he said his dead wife's name. It was as though she meant nothing to him. Or perhaps, Minerva thought slowly, as though he still couldn't bear to think of it, as though the only way he could cope was to tamp the emotions down.

'And what is the horse's name?' she asked quickly.

His brows lifted but he said readily enough, 'Silver Demon.'

Something in her expression must have given her away, because an answering amusement glimmered in his eyes. 'I didn't name him, either. Pretentious, isn't it?'

'It suits him,' she said solemnly, smoothing the soft fur behind Penelope's ears to hide the flutter that smile set up somewhere in the region of her heart.

He shook his head. 'It doesn't. Although he's a stallion he's as placid as a gelding, which is why he's here. We don't breed horses at Spanish Castle, so there's no place for a temperamental stallion, or mare, for that matter; this is a working station.' He paused, then added without expression, 'He doesn't come inside, either.'

When Minerva laughed he watched her with an arrested expression, almost as though a laughing woman was a novelty. The amusement died in her throat. Abruptly, Nick turned towards the door. Answering the unspoken summons, she left Penelope in charge and followed him from the kitchen.

'I'll take you round the ground floor first,' he said, 'so you know your way about, then I'll show you your room.'

The homestead was magnificent, furniture and fabric and the house itself combining to make a harmonious whole. The last room they went into was a splendid dining-room where an eighteenth-century mahogany table was set off perfectly by buttercup-coloured walls and a huge painting that should have been incongruous, a modern South American acrylic of the jungle. Yet the lush, almost naïve picture set off the big room and its elegant, traditional furniture with style and wit.

Gazing around, Minerva asked, 'Who decorated the house? It's brilliant.'

'My mother.'

Was his mother still alive? Yes, Stella had written of a tall, charming woman who had married again. 'She has great talent.'

'Yes,' he said. 'Although most of the furniture was in the house, she re-organised the place to within an inch of its life as well as choosing the colours and the materials. In her day it wasn't done for a young woman to have a career, but she'd have been a success as a decorator. She lives in Singapore now with her second husband, and is having the time of her life redoing his house and garden.'

The stairs led to a passage lit by an arched window above the staircase and a large double-hung window at the other end of the house. More pictures were displayed along the walls, some by artists Minerva thought she recognised, some unknown, but all chosen with discernment and the passion of the true connoisseur.

'Did your mother collect the pictures?' she asked, looking at one particularly impressive oil of a woman on the beach.

'Some. My grandparents and great-grandparents bought some, and I've added to them.'

'They have...' Struggling for a way to express her feelings, she could only say lamely, 'They seem to go to together, to make up a whole.'

'Perhaps because we've only ever bought what we really like,' he said.

Her room, just around the corner from the stairs, was surprisingly large, with a four-poster bed against one wall and a small door opposite. Going over to the bed, Nick turned down the spread.

'It's not made up,' he said. 'I'll help you do it now.'

'I'll do it,' she said swiftly. It was ridiculous, but she didn't want him making the bed with her. 'Where's the linen cupboard?'

He nodded towards a massive French armoire on one wall. 'In there. Are you sure? I do know how to make a bed.'

Minerva's smile was hurried. 'I'm sure you can, but honestly, it's no trouble.'

'All right. The bathroom is through the door beside it,' he said. 'Let me know if there's anything else you want.'

Minerva looked away. The ripple of taut muscle as he swung her pack on to a chair set uneasy excitement singing through her. 'I will,' she said. 'What time do you have dinner?'

'Seven-thirty. I think Helen has left a sort of menu.'

'Yes.'

He said without emotion, 'Thank you for stepping into the breach. Helen was frantic to get to her daughter, but she wouldn't have left me in the lurch.'

'That's loyalty,' Minerva said slowly. Was the housekeeper devoted enough to answer a lawyer who asked questions about the relationship between husband and wife with, if not lies, at least a bending of the truth that favoured her employer?

After all, it would be pragmatic of her to be generous in her interpretation of the situation, even a little biased. Not only did Nick own Spanish Castle, he had interests in other businesses, mostly concerned with the agricultural and pastoral sector, including one entirely successful one he'd set up himself. Irritated by the lack of decent software for agricultural use, he had designed his own, marketed it, and now headed a firm which was expanding its exports by a quantum leap each year.

So he was clever, a creative thinker and an astute businessman as well as part of New Zealand's landed gentry. The Peveril name was one to reckon with in the north. Nick was a local grandee, a power in the country. And he was kind; his concern for Mrs Borrows hadn't been assumed.

Perhaps no one was all that interested in why his wife had died, especially as he hadn't been there when Stella swallowed her deadly mixture of pills.

Nick's broad shoulders moved a fraction. 'She adored my mother,' he said calmly, as though this explained everything. 'Now, about payment. Family or not,' his voice turned sardonic, 'I certainly don't expect you to give up your holiday without making it worthwhile for you.'

Minerva lifted ironic eyes. 'The family bit cuts both ways,' she said lightly, hiding even from herself her instinctive rejection of the idea of taking money from him. 'You don't pay family for coming to the rescue. It isn't done.'

The cold fire of his gaze held hers for a pulse-thudding moment. He meant to ride roughshod over her; she could see his intention as clearly as though he had spoken the words.

Then something changed his mind and his expression altered into the chilly impersonality she was beginning to dislike. With a narrow, sharp-edged smile, he said, 'Very well.'

Oddly enough, she resented his easy capitulation. She had, she realised, looked forward to crossing swords with him. Something told her that he would be a good enemy, hard but just, and that there would be an intense exhilaration in battling him. Minerva rather enjoyed a fair fight; in that she was completely different from Stella, who had hated quarrels and been unable to cope with them.

It seemed suddenly disloyal to bandy words and fence for position with the man who had been instrumental in some way for her sister's death. Her lips tightened. She said too loudly, 'Well, that's settled then. I'd better unpack.'

When he had left the room she stood for a moment, her eyes fixed on the door, before breathing out with a sudden, explosive sound. Then she walked across to the wide bed and sat down on it, her eyes troubled.

He was too much, too tall, too good-looking, with eyes that saw too much and a mouth that promised too much, and a voice that sent too many shivers down her spine. Yet that uncompromising dominance wasn't entirely physical; even curbed by will-power, the dark force of his personality blazed forth with an indelible impact. No wonder Stella had been overwhelmed.

More than anything, Minerva wanted to understand her stepsister's state of mind in those last months before her death. Oh, she hadn't come up here deliberately to spy and poke and probe, but that had to be part of the reason she had turned off Highway 10 and headed up the hill. For a year Stella's death had nagged at her, demanding that she do something about it, that she make someone suffer for it.

She needed to find out what had driven her stepsister to take that final, irrevocable step into the darkness. If they knew, Ruth and her father could pick up the threads of their lives and find some measure of serenity and acceptance.

Initially she had blamed Nick, but now it seemed fairly clear that like Ruth, like them all, he was living in one of the darker corners of hell.

Minerva sighed, looking around with a troubled frown.

Perhaps Stella should be allowed to rest in peace, that lovely phrase which promised so much.

Biting her lip, Minerva stared down at the faded hues of the Persian carpet, watching the wonderful coppery red and brilliant blue blur through her tears into a jumble of undefined hues.

What had been Stella's thoughts during the last night she had spent here?

No one, she thought sadly, would ever know. Stella had made sure of that by not asking for help, by giving no reason. Sometimes Minerva wondered whether she would have made a difference; whether, if she'd been home, Stella would have confided in her.

Although Minerva was a year younger, she had been the stronger, treading through the minefields of adolescence with a light foot and comparative ease, whereas Stella had made hard weather of it.

When Stella got drunk it had been Minerva who had smuggled her into the house and dealt with the aftermath, just as she had coped the time Stella had tried marijuana. Later, realising that Stella had embarked on the first of a series of affairs, it was Minerva who had expostulated. Stella had listened, said airily that making love with someone you liked was no big deal, and not let Minerva's reasoned arguments affect her behaviour at all.

In spite of her light-heartedness and her fragility, Stella had never been one for confidences. Minerva's hands clenched on her lap as she fought guilt and pain and a wasteland of emotions. Why should she think that she might have made a difference if Ruth hadn't seen anything, if Nick had been unable to help the woman he had married, the woman who had loved him so desperately? Although it hurt to accept that there was probably nothing she could have done, she had to, or risk spending the rest of her life haunted by regret.

It was time to let the past bury its dead.

Wearily, she went into the bathroom, a room of Victorian splendour, claw-footed bath and all, only modernised in the most essential ways. As warm and dry as the rest of the house, it breathed the same indefinable air of luxury.

Staring into the well-lit mirror, she saw no ghosts, just her own somewhat plain reflection, its only claims to beauty a heart-shaped face and a pair of large, dark blue eyes set in thick black lashes.

Stella had been a golden girl, with skin that tanned easily into a warm brilliance, set off by soft blue eyes and curly amber hair.

When Minerva was growing up she had hated her pallor and the sudden contrast of eyes and lashes and full, red mouth. After the affair with Paul she'd become reconciled to her lack of beauty. Her first and only romance had taught her that, when it came to looks versus character in women, looks won out every time.

Her hands fell to her side. Mouth twisting into a cynical little smile, she recalled unflinchingly Paul's voice as he had pointed out her deficiencies in that department. She only had herself to blame; stupidly, she had pleaded with him to tell her why he was leaving. So he had.

'Don't you ever look at yourself in the mirror? You're too thin, and you don't make enough of what you have got—you dress as though you're ashamed of being a woman.'

Stung, she had countered, 'Just because I don't wear plunging necklines——'

'Well, darling, you haven't got anything to plunge to, have you? Nice enough in their little way, but it's a *very* little way, isn't it?'

She understood now that he had been angry because she had forced him to justify his betrayal, but then his acid irritation had humiliated her.

He had looked at her white face and said shamefacedly, 'I'm sorry, Minerva, I don't want to hurt you, we've had some good times together, but when I saw Cass again, I knew that—well, that's all they were, good times.'

She had thought Paul loved her as much as she loved him. Lord, but she'd been green, too green to realise that Paul had been using her to make his girlfriend jealous. Even more than his casual dismissal of her physical attributes and the lovemaking they had shared, she'd been wounded by her own stupidity.

The humiliation had long gone; within three months his pretty, voluptuous Cass had dumped him for a tall footballer. Now Minerva knew he'd been immature and cruelly spoilt, but the whole episode had left her with a cynicism that her life cooking meals for the rich had intensified.

Oh, she believed in love; only death had severed her father's love for her mother, and his second marriage was truly happy, too. But if and when she married it would not be under the spell of a chemistry so intense she mistook it for love.

'Never,' she said, shaking her head.

The forgotten locks of hair moved in a rippling mass. She pulled a face at the determined woman in the mirror and set to tidying herself. Her long-fingered hands moved swiftly, pinning the strands to the back of her head. Although the style was severely practical, just as practical as her hands and her skills, it made her look older and more severe.

That, she thought as she turned to make the bed, was how she was. Her hard-won peace of mind was not going to be in jeopardy because the man who had married Stella looked like a fallen angel.

When Nick came into the kitchen just before half-past four, Minerva was taking a tray of muffins from the oven. Acutely aware of his burnished glance, she flicked them on to a wire rack and covered them with a cloth.

His smile, swift and brilliant as a lightning flash, seared through her. 'Are those for afternoon tea? They smell good.'

Something moved in the pit of her stomach, primeval, intense. 'Yes,' she said shortly.

The telephone interrupted. He answered it, asked a couple of questions, said, 'I'll ring you back in five minutes when I've got the information,' and hung up, asking, 'Is the tea made?'

'No, I've only just put the kettle on.'

'In that case, can you bring it to the office?'

'Yes, of course.'

The office was a large room with a very intimidating computer set-up. Minerva, who had a novice's fear of technology, put the tray down on one corner of the desk well away from it, and turned to go.

Nick was reading something at the desk, his lean hand making quick notes in the margin. Apart from calling 'Come in,' when she knocked, he hadn't looked up. But as she moved away, he asked absently, 'Why is there only one cup and saucer?'

'Well, I——'

He lifted his head, his eyes narrowing. 'Go and get another cup for yourself.'

Another direct order, and one that he didn't expect to be disobeyed. He didn't seem to realise that she might prefer some privacy. Minerva hesitated.

There was no warmth in his eyes, yet she thought they lingered a moment on her mouth. 'Minerva,' he said softly, 'you're here as a member of the family who is helping out, not as a hired hand. You said so, remember.'

She returned defensively, 'After five years of being very much the hired help, being a member of the family is going to take a bit of getting used to.'

'Get used to it,' he commanded as she turned to leave the room. 'You're doing both Helen and me a favour.'

When she returned he was still scribbling notes in the margin, but as she came into the room he put his pen down and stood up, waiting for her to sit down.

'Have you got yourself organised?' he asked quite pleasantly.

'Oh, yes.' Far too aware of him, she poured the tea and set the pot down. In spite of his superficial pleasantness there was something curiously implacable about Nick Peveril.

'Can you cope with the menu for the dinner?'

'That's no problem.' She could cope with an infinitely more elaborate menu than the one Helen had made out, but she wasn't going to tell him that. It sounded too much like boasting, and he wasn't her employer; she didn't have to impress him with her skill. She said, 'I'll need some help, though. I can cook it, but I'm not going to be able to serve a sit-down meal for twenty people by myself.'

'That's all organised. Jillian Howard's going to be here all of Friday and Saturday; she'll help in the kitchen with the dinner, and the two high-school sons of the head shepherd will serve at table.'

Minerva knew she looked taken aback. Composing her expression, she asked, 'Do they know what they're doing?'

'Yes, they've done it before. I prefer to get people who are working on the station to help out.'

It sounded very worthy, although Minerva caught herself wondering whether they were too intimidated by the man to refuse.

'You, of course, will eat with us,' he said, so blandly that she wondered for one heart-stopping moment whether he was able to read her thoughts.

She frowned. 'It will make things more difficult,' she warned.

His brows lifted slightly. 'Too difficult?'

'Well, no,' she admitted.

'Good. I'd like you to act as my hostess.'

'Oh, but——' Minerva's eyes met his. She could read nothing in their depths, but her protest died before Genevieve Chatswood's name fell from her unruly tongue.

'That's settled, then. Is there anything else you want to know?' he asked politely.

She shook her head. 'Not at the moment, no.'

Leaning forward, he said, 'I know I more or less dumped you in it, and I'm damned grateful. Helen wouldn't have gone if you hadn't agreed, and, to be honest, I didn't like the sound of her daughter's condition.'

Minerva said quietly, 'I hope she's all right. As for the other—well, it was good luck that I happened to be here. Perhaps it was meant.'

'Or perhaps just coincidence,' he countered, sounding very slightly bored. 'Do you like what you've seen of the north so far?'

'All I've seen so far,' she told him acidly, 'is rain. I left Auckland on a glorious day, but as soon as I reached the Brynderwyn Hills the rain set in, and it's been raining on and off ever since.'

'Well, you would come up in spring. Look at it this way—things can only get better. Last summer was such a dreary one we're hoping for a good warm season this year. That's if Mount Pinatubo in the Philippines doesn't blow again.'

'I thought farmers hated lovely dry summers,' she said contrarily.

'Who said anything about dry? A summer with no wind and at least an inch of rain each week will do us fine. Although there's always the possibility of facial eczema then, of course.'

Minerva smiled. 'I knew there had to be some catch,' she teased. 'Farmers are notorious for never being happy.'

'Only because so much can go wrong when you're at the mercy of the weather,' he parried, a glint of amusement softening his features. 'Cyclones, hailstorms, floods——'

'Floods? Up here on the top of a thumping great hill?'

'You'd be surprised how flooded the creek can get. We're high enough to collect any raincloud that's crossing Northland so we have to watch it carefully.'

The telephone rang. As he answered it Minerva started to get to her feet, but he shook his head. His hair gleamed golden in the light of the businesslike lamp above the desk. 'Frank—what——? Where is he?'

The telephone quacked on. Nick frowned, staring into space, his eyes as clear and cold as shards of diamond. 'No, I'm having afternoon tea. I'll finish that, then go. I don't care if he is wet!' He hung up.

Minerva tried to look blank as though Frank and his wetness didn't interest her in the least.

'Frank is the other stockman,' he said blandly, reaching for a muffin. Strong white teeth bit into it.

Minerva knew she was an excellent cook, but she held her breath as he ate it, only relaxing when he said somewhat thickly, 'This is delicious.'

'Thank you.' Curiosity overcame discretion. 'Why is Frank wet?'

'Today's his day off and he's been down at the pub since it opened. He decided not to drive his car home, so he started to walk. That was the manager's wife. She's just come back from shopping and picking up the kids at school. She offered Frank a ride, but he said he wasn't fit to be in the car with children. Which is true—he's drunk. So I'll have to pick him up before the idiot gets run over.'

Minerva's astonishment showed in her expression.

'Good help is hard to get,' he said shortly. 'It's the isolation.'

Clearly he had a paternalistic attitude towards his workers. No doubt the less ambitious liked it. It would have irked Minerva no end, but then, she had fought for her independence. Ruth had been horrified when she'd insisted on training as a chef. Her stepmother was a darling, but she was a little snobbish, and the thought of a member of her family working 'as a servant' had been hard to swallow.

Had Minerva taken Ruth's tempting bait, sweetened with love and security, comfort and laughter, she would have stayed at home in a nice, safe job that didn't take any of her energies, until she married. Like Stella.

'The isolation?' she asked now. 'What isolation, for heaven's sake?'

Nick leaned back in his chair and looked at her as though the slight snap in her voice intrigued him. 'You don't think you'll mind the isolation?'

'We're only about twenty kilometres from Kerikeri. I don't call that isolated.'

'It's a state of mind rather than a distance,' he said.

Something in his voice caught Minerva's attention. Hidden beneath the cool, distancing tone was a thread of intensity, a cryptic combination that sent small shocks along her nerve-ends. She looked up at an expressionless face, into eyes that seemed transparent as well-water, at a mouth relaxed into a crooked half-smile, yet she felt some unfathomable force beating through that enigmatic composure like the throb of a distant drum.

'Yes, I suppose you're right,' she said quietly, more to fill the pulsing silence than to make a point. 'My idea of isolation is somewhere the mail doesn't go.'

Dark brows were raised. 'We get it six times a week,' he said, dead-pan.

'How about your television reception?'

'Perfect.'

'And you've got power and water, as well as at least two bookshops in Kerikeri. A cinema, too. I don't think you're isolated at all. This is civilisation compared to some of the places I've been.'

His smile was ironic, almost mocking. 'How adaptable you are. Where have you been?'

'Oh, all around,' she said vaguely, and picked up her cup and saucer again. People who boasted of their travels were complete bores.

He nodded, the dazzling eyes holding hers for a second until he reached for another muffin.

'I'd better get back to the kitchen,' she said, getting to her feet. He looked at her as though he knew she was retreating, and that slightly lop-sided mouth twisted.

'Thank you again,' he said as he rose. He waited until she was at the door before saying lightly, 'Minerva?'

She looked over her shoulder. 'Yes?'

'Welcome to Spanish Castle.'

It almost sounded like a warning. She asked quickly, 'Why Spanish? I can see the Castle, but it doesn't look any more like a Spanish castle than an English one.'

'Have you never heard of castles in Spain? Airy, insubstantial, glamorous illusions that fade with the hard light of day? You dream about your castle in Spain, but you never get it. A hundred and fifty years ago Nicholas

Peveril came here with a woman he stole. He was happy for a little while, but he always knew her husband would find them. Which he did, after she'd spent two years in Nicholas's bed and given him a son.'

'He *stole* her?'

'Remind me to tell you the whole story one day.' That infuriating indifference had returned.

He nodded dismissively and turned back to the work he had been doing when she came in, his lean, strong hand moving decisively in the margin, the black writing standing out stark and very clear against the white paper.

'Oh, by the way,' he said without looking at her, 'you'd better ring your parents to let them know where you are. If I know Ruth, she'll have made you promise to ring every day, anyway.'

'She tried,' she said ironically. 'You know Ruth. Five years of looking after myself count for nothing when I land in New Zealand, possibly the safest place in the world.'

'Unfortunately, we've not been able to buck the trends. There are murderers and rapists here too,' he said calmly.

'I know. And sometimes there's a person whose only mistake is being in the wrong place at the wrong time. But all the telephone calls home are not going to make any difference, so I keep telling Ruth. So far I haven't been able to convince her! I will ring her tonight, even if it's only to make her feel happier. Thanks.'

He left almost immediately on his mission of mercy, so Minerva was able to relax as she peeled the ends of a fat bunch of asparagus, freshly cut from a garden somewhere close by.

It was strange in the big house by herself, with only Penelope, relaxed on the chair, for company. Accustomed to locks and keys and guards, to the strict security of a world gone mad, Minerva wondered at the man who would leave a total stranger here among so many beautiful things, and apparently not worry in the least about it.

She could have been a complete opportunist; she needn't really be Stella's sister. Nick obviously hadn't recognised her. She was surprised to find that this hurt, a tiny niggling ache, and recognised it for the danger signal it was.

Nick Peveril might be a cold fish, but he was a very attractive cold fish, with far more than his share of a profound male magnetism that seemed to have absolutely nothing to do with character or worth. Purely physical...

And perhaps he wasn't so cold, after all. If anyone had asked her she wouldn't have believed that he would drive through the rain to pick up his drunk stockman.

He arrived back within the hour, but stayed in the office. Minerva gave a final look around the kitchen, satisfied herself that her preparations for the meal were well under control, and went upstairs to shower and change.

Fortunately, in spite of the fact that she had planned to stay in motels and eat mostly takeaways, she had brought two all-purpose, almost uncrushable dresses that rolled up into no space at all. They were hardly glamorous, but they'd do. She eyed them both. One was the soft, clear ice-pink that suited her so well, the other the axiomatic little black dress. Deciding on the black, she hung it in the bathroom while she showered so the steam could smooth out its few creases. It was ready when, after putting on the lipstick and blusher that was all she used, she got into it.

Nick gave her a glass of sherry before dinner; they talked of her parents and her half-brother Kane, who was enjoying himself enormously at the same boarding-school Nick had attended, then found themselves discussing the implications of a book that had startled New Zealand. It was pleasant and low-key, and Minerva didn't drink all of her sherry, yet she felt as though it had been champagne. Tiny bubbles of excitement fizzed softly through her bloodstream.

They ate in the morning-room off the kitchen, a room that moonlighted as a sitting-room too, for there were comfortable chairs at one end, and a set of cabinets and shelves that held books and pretty things as well as a television and an imposing stereo and CD player. The billionaire had been a stereo buff; Minerva noticed that the name on the speakers was the one on the huge affairs in the yacht.

Over dinner they spoke of generalities, nothing personal. Nick's conversation revealed an incisive brain and a crisply unsentimental outlook which Minerva rather liked. She enjoyed the way he put her on her mettle.

Afterwards he helped carry the dishes into the kitchen, stacked the dishwasher while she made coffee, and told her that she was to feel free to watch television or play music if she wanted to. Unfortunately he wasn't going to be able to stay with her; he had more work to get through.

Minerva found herself wondering if the detachment she found so off-putting was merely a front he assumed. Intuition, that subliminal reading of unnoticeable signs and intonations, made her suspect him of being a man of strong emotions and intense desires.

Of course she could be wrong. Perhaps he was simply ice through and through, and poor Stella had frozen to death.

She drank her coffee with him, and when he had gone back to the office rang her parents in their hotel in Seattle.

'You're *where*?' Ruth asked.

'Spanish Castle.' She was glad Nick had left the room, because there was a note of betraying self-consciousness in her voice that galled her. 'I dropped in to see Mr—Nick, just as his housekeeper was called away on a family emergency. She didn't think she could go because Nick's having a group of very high-powered Brazilian officials to dinner on Saturday, so Nick co-opted me.'

'That's sweet of you,' Ruth said with satisfaction. 'But talk about a busman's holiday!'

'I do like cooking, you know.'

'Just as well, isn't it. Darling, is Nick there with you?'

Absently, Minerva shook her head. 'No, he's working in his office.'

'Oh, I won't disturb him then.'

Ruth liked talking on the telephone, but eventually Minerva said, 'Ruth, I have to go. This is costing me a packet!'

'Surely Nick will——'

Minerva said firmly, 'I'm paying for it.'

'All right, then, I'll see you when we get home, darling. Don't hurry back to Auckland, though, if you're having fun at Spanish Castle.'

Fun! Oh, Ruth, if you only knew, Minerva thought as she hung up.

On her way to bed, Minerva hesitated. Should she just go up, or beard the lion in his den and say goodnight? Bearding the lion seemed more polite. He might growl at her interruption, but Ruth would be proud of her manners.

He didn't growl, or show any claws. Reading the contents of a file, he was standing across the room by a bank of cabinets. Even after he looked up it took a moment for him to register that she was there. 'Yes?' he said curtly.

'I'm on my way to bed.' A yawn brought her hand up over her mouth. 'What time do you eat breakfast?'

'Seven o'clock, but don't worry about getting up, I can make my own. Goodnight. And thank you very much for stepping into the breach like this.' His face was expressionless, his voice cool and distant.

'Families are wonderful institutions,' she returned flippantly. 'Goodnight.'

The rain had stopped during dinner, and with a lightning change of mood the weather had gone from dank to fine. Up in her room, Minerva got into her pyjamas then sat on the bed, listening to the quietness flow in through the windows and through the big house. Nothing stirred; there was no sound of traffic, no breath of wind, nothing but peace and a cool, dark, moonless tranquillity.

Stella had loved parties and dances and dinners, people and motion and music; how had she felt about this all-pervading silence?

Yawning, Minerva got into bed and stretched out luxuriously across the queensized innersprung mattress.

She was almost asleep when she heard Nick come along the passage past her door. For a moment she thought he had stopped outside her room, but no, of course he'd gone into the room next door. It gave her the oddest sensation. The walls were too thick for her to hear more than the occasional noise of movement, but she could imagine him stripping off and getting into bed, and her wayward brain didn't want to stop there.

Well, why not? she thought, trying to make light of it. Nick Peveril was definitely fantasy material, if you could put up with the icy remoteness.

Later, waking up from a confused dream, she realised she'd seen nothing of Stella in the grand old house, no photograph in the morning-room, nothing to say she had lived there. It seemed that, as far as Spanish Castle was concerned, her stepsister had simply never existed.

CHAPTER THREE

IN THE morning Minerva woke to a terrifying sense of dislocation. For a moment she lay staring at the ornately pleated silk of the tester above her, until she remembered where she was.

Reluctantly, she got out of the comfortable bed and pulled back the curtains, to gaze disbelievingly at a day as glowing and peerless as anything summer itself could produce.

Spiders' webs looped crystal netting along the wire fence; she looked beyond gardens and trees and thickly wooded paddocks to darkly brooding bush. A blazing silver arc across the eastern horizon indicated the distant sea.

Minerva had gloried in beauty before, had chosen her jobs for their superb surroundings, but Spanish Castle on a fine spring morning took her breath away. Smiling at the sight of a blackbird tugging ferociously on a worm in the lawn below, she watched it almost land on its feathered rump. Its subsequent ridiculous look of embarrassment summoned soft laughter.

When she'd washed her face and cleaned her teeth she climbed into jeans, a shirt and a warm sweatshirt and headed down the stairs. To her astonishment Nick was already on his way out of the house. Surely he hadn't had his breakfast! A quick look around the pristine kitchen reassured her.

After a brief exchange of greetings she asked in a husky morning voice, 'What do you have for breakfast?'

He shrugged. 'Anything you like to cook. Cereal and toast will do. I'll feed the dogs first.'

'How long will you be?'

'Five minutes at the outside.'

Without further questions she prepared a substantial breakfast of bacon and tomatoes, with toast and orange juice and coffee.

When he'd finished he remarked with an air of mild surprise, 'That was good.'

'Thank you,' she said acerbically.

He grinned. 'I'm sorry. You just don't seem old enough to be able to cook like a dream. With your hair dragged behind your face like that you look about sixteen.'

In her gruffest voice, she said, 'Well, I'm not.'

'Are you a night person, Minerva?'

'Yes, although early morning is my favourite time of day. It just takes me a while to get my tongue into working order. You'll get used to me.'

'I doubt it.'

His dry tone caught her attention. Refusing to wonder what it meant, she continued making steady inroads into her cereal and orange juice. Even at this hour of the morning she was far too conscious of his powerful magnetism. His vital male presence set off unwanted, unfortunate responses all through her.

Making a great effort to achieve something like her normal animation, she asked, 'Will you be in for morning tea and lunch?'

'No. I have a meeting in Whangarei that's likely to go on all afternoon, so I probably won't be back until after six. Don't forget Jillian Howard will be here at nine.'

'What does she do?'

He looked slightly startled. 'I don't know. Mops and dusts and washes, that sort of thing. Helen does the lighter stuff. A firm of commercial cleaners from Kerikeri deals with the windows, and once a year the place is spring cleaned.' That tilted smile appeared. 'Usually when I'm away, I'm thankful to say.'

Minerva knew all about that. The employer was always spared the worst bits of housecleaning. She said, 'Well, what exactly do you want me to do?'

His brows drew together. 'I thought we'd settled this. You're not an employee, you're a member of the family, so you do exactly what you want to do. Would you like to come to Whangarei with me today?'

A quick surge of anticipation was instantly dammed. 'No, thanks. I need to wash a few clothes.'

'Of course.' He paused, then finished, 'Don't feel obliged to do any more than you want to.'

She nodded, trying not to feel as though she'd just had a long-promised treat cancelled. Damn it, she didn't want to go to Whangarei with him. Common sense had won out over irresponsibility.

Unfortunately, the niggle of disappointment didn't go away. In a subtle, not easily discerned way, he posed a threat to her. The previous night, just before she'd slid into sleep, she had wondered whether her decision to leave Stella to her rest might have had something to do with meeting this man.

Now she knew it had, and the knowledge stung.

She couldn't afford to develop a fixation on him. It hadn't done Stella any good, she thought, as she nodded and said, 'I won't, don't worry,' trying with a faintly ridiculous caution to set him at a distance.

Yet why should she be suspicious? No one else seemed to be. He was on excellent terms with Ruth and Brian; everyone felt sorry for the widower whose wife had suddenly, for no apparent reason, committed suicide.

It came too easily to him, she thought crossly as she began to tidy the kitchen. He was—oh, he knew damned well he had only to smile at a woman, only to look at her with those speculative silver eyes to activate the tingle at the base of her spine, the primal, passionate reaction to his forceful masculine sexuality. Utterly male, intensely confident, he was compellingly attractive.

Her thoughts turned acid. Not only did he know it, but it meant nothing to him.

* * *

Jillian Howard was young and brisk and cheerful, and within half an hour proved that she was efficient and hardworking.

She was also a gossip. As they drank morning tea together she gave an unwilling Minerva a quick, lightly malicious rundown on all the staff at the station, then put her through a polite grilling. Circumventing her obvious intention of gathering as much information as she could to pass on, Minerva told her anecdotes that were funny, or dramatic, or both.

Round-eyed and entranced, Jillian was impressed. 'What actor?' she asked eagerly at the end of one particularly juicy tale. 'Come on, Minerva, who was he?'

Minerva grinned. 'Sorry,' she said, 'but one day I might want to work for him, and if he ever found out I'd been telling tales out of school, bang would go my reputation for discretion.'

'Oh, it must be neat, living like that.' Jillian sighed enviously. 'What are they like, really rich people?'

Minerva shrugged. 'Much the same as really poor people. The main difference is that rich people have more comfortable surroundings to be happy or miserable in.' She was going to add that Nick was probably as rich as anyone she'd worked for, but common sense warned her away from the subject.

Or perhaps it was instinct, for at that moment Jill looked up and said in an altered voice, 'Oh, hi, Nick. Minerva's just been telling me fascinating stories about actors and millionaires, but she won't tell me who they are.'

Dressed to go out, he was wearing well-cut trousers and a sports coat that had been tailored with the express design of showing off his wide shoulders and narrow waist to their best advantage.

His smile was impartially divided between both women. 'I imagine discretion is essential in her profession,' he said mildly. 'Have you seen Frank this morning?'

'Yeah, he came over for breakfast the same as usual.'
Something wasn't quite right with Jillian's smile. 'He
looked a bit grotty, but he's OK.'

'Good. I'll see you later,' he said to Minerva, and left.

When he was safely out of hearing, Jillian sighed.
'God, he's gorgeous, isn't he? What a hunk! He makes
my backbone go all funny when he looks at me.' She
stopped, and looked through her lashes at Minerva.
'Oops,' she said, 'I keep forgetting you're his sister-in-
law.'

Nick had made sure the younger woman knew that
Minerva was Stella's sister; no doubt safeguarding his
reputation, she thought ironically. Aloud, she said, 'I
imagine he has that effect on most women.'

'Well, he *is* luscious, isn't he? A bit aloof, but definitely the sort of man you dream about just before you
go to sleep. And that stand-offish air makes him all the
more interesting, if you know what I mean. You can't
imagine him letting down his guard at all, can you? Mind
you,' she murmured, looking at Minerva through her
lashes, 'he's got the devil's temper.'

Astonished, Minerva said, 'Nick?'

'Yeah, Nick.' Like all gossips, Jillian was pleased with
the surprise her comment had roused. 'Oh, he's not
peppery, he doesn't fly off the handle all the time. He's
got a slow fuse, but when it's lit——' she made a graphic
gesture '—man, watch out! Frank told us once that he
saw Nick lose his temper with a stockman who used a
whip on his dog. Frank said he broke the guy's jaw and
told him to get off the place and never come back again.'

'Broke his jaw?' Minerva protested. '*Nick*? Oh, come
on now!'

'No, it's true. You ask around; everyone who knows
him says he takes a long time to blow, but when it
happens—boom! Like a volcano. It's run-for-cover time.'

Minerva had guessed that the self-command which
disciplined his emotions was merely an armour. Was that
what had happened to Stella, who hated fights or quarrels

or confrontations? Had she been so frightened by a display of temper——? No, Stella hadn't been a *wimp*. She'd have left him and gone home, not killed herself.

And Minerva wasn't going to listen to any more gossip about Nick, either. She said, 'I suppose we'd better get on.'

'OK. I'll do the dusting. I see you're in your sister's room, now. She liked that bed. Great style, she used to say.'

'I like it, too.' Sister's room? Hadn't they slept together? A complex mix of emotions swirled through Minerva.

Apparently not noticing, Jillian said earnestly, 'I was sorry about your sister. She was nice, but she didn't seem happy here.' There was no mistaking her sincerity. 'I got on well with her—I suppose because we were the youngest wives on the station, and we were both exiles.'

Stella had enjoyed her hectic social life, but surely she'd realised that it would be different in the country? A peculiar coldness iced through Minerva's stomach. If anyone knew what had driven Stella to take that final step it could be the woman who was rinsing her mug out in the sink.

'I thought she liked living here,' Minerva remarked casually.

'No.' Jillian's tone was definite. 'Well, it stands to reason! I get bored to screaming point sometimes, and I grew up on a farm! I only lived in Auckland a year, but I loved it, all the restaurants and nightclubs and pubs, there's always something to do. I didn't want to leave. Your sister really missed it; she used to go down as often as she could. Spanish Castle must have seemed like the end of the world.'

'If you get so bored, what you are doing here?' Minerva made her voice idle, only vaguely interested.

Jillian shrugged, her eyes gleaming catlike beneath darkened lashes. 'It's a career move. Nick helps good workers with finance for their own farms.' Jillian took out a teatowel and dried her mug, her vigorous movements adding emphasis to her words. 'I'm not going to spend the rest of my life living in a farmworker's cottage and cleaning up the homestead and cooking for hungover stockmen.'

'Nick sounds like a good boss.'

The younger woman shrugged. 'Good as any, I suppose, better than a lot. He'll do anything for you, Nick will, if you're prepared to work. But he's a hard man; anyone who doesn't work gets dumped.'

Minerva said mildly, 'Yet he went down to pick up Frank whoever-he-is after he'd been at the pub all day. That doesn't sound like a hard man.'

'Oh, Frank!' She sounded scornful and pitying together. 'He's a mess. His wife's just taken off with their two little kids, and Frank's in a real state. Nick has been pretty good to him; he suggested I cook for him, but I reckon his patience is just about used up. And if Frank lay in bed with a hangover after each bender he'd be down the road quick and busy. Nick likes his pound of flesh.'

She put the mug into the cupboard and turned around so that she could see Minerva's face when she finished, 'I wouldn't be surprised if Frank's not going the same way as your sister, heading for a breakdown. I suggested he see someone, but he hit the roof. You can't tell some people. They won't listen, and they won't take help.'

'Did you suggest Stella get help?' Minerva asked gently.

Jillian hesitated, and Minerva went on, 'Because if you did, thank you.'

The young, sharp, oddly hungry face eased. 'Yeah, well, I did. I mean, I could tell she wasn't happy, although she was good at hiding her feelings. I didn't realise she was at the end of her tether until only a week before she d— passed away. I found her crying in the car. She'd just come back from the doctor, and I don't know what he told her, but she was heartbroken.'

'Thank you for trying to help,' Minerva said, steadying her voice with an effort. At the inquest nobody had mentioned anything about a visit to the doctor.

Jillian shrugged. 'I felt sorry for her,' she said, gathering up a tin of beeswax and several dusters. 'I mean, she had everything—didn't she?—and I've got nothing, but she was crying hard enough to choke herself. And when I told her to tell Nick, she just about had a fit. "No, not Nick", she said, as though she was frightened he'd eat her. Funny, wasn't it? Because they seemed happy enough. Although——' She hesitated, obviously on the brink of saying something else.

Minerva tried to look as unthreatening and encouraging as possible, but the moment for confidences had fled. Jillian's withdrawal was palpable, so Minerva asked, 'Did you tell Nick about this? After she died, I mean.'

'Oh, yes, I told him. He already knew all about it. He said it was nothing.' Clearly he hadn't convinced her. 'Well, I'd better get back to work, I suppose.'

She left at twelve. After a scrappy lunch Minerva went out for a walk, passing the two dogs lying in the sun outside their kennels beside the garage. They looked eagerly at her and wagged their tails in what she construed to be a hopeful manner.

She patted each narrow, intelligent head, but said, 'I'd let you come with me, but I don't know whether you're allowed off.'

Rusty gave himself a smart scratch, then lay down, head on his paws, clearly not expecting a walk. Smiling, Minerva set off along the drive she'd come up the day before. It wound through the thick belt of trees surrounding the garden before emerging into the open at a cattle-stop with a wide gate beside it. A stone wall stretched both ways around the homestead gardens. More stone walls, still in excellent repair although all had two or three strands of barbed wire along the top, divided the paddocks. On the other side of the road the domed, branchy tops of the *kauri* trees in the forest park cut into the sky.

Sleek, ponderous bulls of an unknown breed stood around chewing their cuds and looking virile. Minerva had a town-dweller's respect for large animals, and, when every big-eyed head turned to watch her with definite, although apparently placid interest, she decided she was not going beyond the garden.

Still, it was very pleasant leaning on the wall. The sun shone down with the tender radiance that only spring knows, and everywhere there was green grass and trees and the scent of growing things. The rocky heights of Spanish Castle loomed over the lush pastures, close enough to shelter, too far away to be intimidating, the stern effect of its great crags mitigated by the trees and plants that clung to every crack and fissure.

A man on a tractor gave a lazy wave as he drove down towards a shed. Minerva waved back.

She smiled, but like a dark stain in clear water doubts roiled through her pleasure in the day.

Why had Stella gone to the doctor, and what had he told her? Just as important, why hadn't that piece of information come out at the inquest?

Did medical confidentiality extend to inquests? At the thought of Stella lonely and unhappy, Minerva felt a pang of overwhelming grief. And a kind of nausea. She was not, she thought grimly, the sort of person who enjoyed mysteries and puzzles, especially when the puzzle was someone's misery. And this one was entirely too close to home.

What did she know of Nick, apart from the fact that he was a good employer and a good farmer, strangely guarded and, according to the gossipy Jillian, with a fierce temper that sometimes led to violence? He certainly hadn't been a good husband, or he'd have realised what was happening to his wife.

Jillian's hint about them sleeping in separate rooms fretted at her mind.

In spite of the way he'd taken Helen Borrows in hand and organised her departure to her daughter's bedside, in spite of Stella's ecstatic letters about his wit and style, he seemed fundamentally austere. A man's basic character didn't change. He must have fascinated Stella into believing he was the sort of man she wanted, witty and charming and fun, fundamentally lightweight.

Minerva bit her soft lip. Nick might seem frigidly bloodless, so tightly leashed did he keep his emotions, but his intense masculinity indicated that, although he could control his appetites, he experienced them. And swirling about him like a cloak was an aura of expertise, warning every woman he came in contact with that he was a skilful lover.

For all her experience, Stella had not enjoyed making love. She had once told Minerva that men wanted sex so she gave it to them, but it wasn't much pleasure for women. What she had enjoyed was the flirting beforehand, the cuddles and kisses and the meeting of eyes, the tiny torments and teasing, the significant laughter. The actual consummation had always been a crashing anticlimax. Boring, sex was, she used to say with a grimace always followed by sly, warm laughter: messy and sweaty, and men were always so serious about it!

Had it been like that with Nick? Minerva clamped down on the part of her that shouted *impossible*. Stella had loved Nick, but that didn't necessarily mean a change in her attitude to sex. Had Nick been disappointed, too? Hard men could be frightening, but was he cruel?

Minerva's hand clenched on the rough, lichened stone. Her quick, intense revulsion at the idea set more warning bells jangling. When Nick had appeared like some primitive god of the storm, big, elemental, almost awe-inspiring, some hitherto repressed part of her had responded instantly.

It would be too easy to become emotionally entangled with him, a man she had met only the day before.

A man Minerva Robertson wanted.

There, she had admitted it. She looked down at her hand, flexing long fingers to banish the tension.

Trying to hide from it would only make her more vulnerable, and she couldn't afford to be. She was attracted to a very dangerous man, a man able to keep his emotions prisoner to his will.

The burgeoning physical fascination she could deal with; this need to believe him completely innocent in Stella's death was another thing entirely, potentially far more perilous than the swift, blind hunger for a man of overwhelming sexual charisma.

She took a shallow breath, forcing herself to think past the quiver down her spine, the instinctive knowledge that he would be a dynamic and potent lover. And a good provider, she thought practically: the two things, perhaps, that women had looked for in their men during the long, endless ages when strength and prestige and cunning in her mate meant that a woman's children were more likely to survive to adulthood.

It wasn't like that now, but the past was not so easy to shuck off. His magnetic appeal lay in the uncomplicated power of his masculinity.

And against that basic pull of the senses, she had to set the fact that Nick Peveril was the man who had stood by and let her stepsister kill herself.

Minerva blinked; the smiling land, the trees, the big, ponderous bulls, whirled a moment, then settled down as she forced the tears back. Staring around, she wondered morbidly what secrets lay beneath the surface of Nick's privileged life. Unease crawled with spiky, insect steps across her skin as she also wondered whether Spanish Castle would be as dangerous to her as it had been to Stella.

No. She straightened, took a deep breath. She was going to be sensible. Nick had made such an impression on her that she wasn't seeing things straight, but that would pass. All she had to do was resist her shaming weakness.

Turning away, she walked up the drive towards the homestead.

Presumably Nick's mother had reorganised the garden as well as the house, using the established framework of trees and shrubs. If so, she was as skilled a designer with plants and shrubs as with furniture and pictures. Minerva admired roses and viburnums, the tiny new leaves of budding maples, the gentle charm of daisies and pinks and other cottagey flowers, and the glowing, perfect blooms of the last of the camellias.

Some distance from the homestead, among banks of azaleas and rhododendrons, she found a path that led between massive *puriri* and *totara* trees, past tree ferns and *nikau* palms and fuchsia bushes, to a swimming-pool.

Here everything was exotically different, the subtropical heritage of the north openly stated. Minerva stood beneath a magnificent jacaranda tree and gazed around at the brilliant, surreal flowers of kangaroo paw in massed plantings, bold scarlet and purple sparaxias and babianas, the white clumps of arum lilies and the almost violently vivid colours and shapes of bromeliads.

They would have been too alien against the Victorian gingerbread of the homestead, but segregated like this, set off by the spiky leaves and subdued colours of New Zealand flax bushes and the white, heavily scented trumpet flowers of a *datura* tree, the huge rocky ramparts of the Spanish Castle looming behind, they were completely at home.

A wide building, its veranda shaded by jasmine and bougainvillaea, stretched behind the still, dark pool. In the beds that linked pool, terrace and poolhouse together there were pawpaws and hibiscus and plumbago bushes, looking a little tired after winter but with new growth showing on the twigs and branches. Palms added an even more tropical air.

Minerva drew a deep, delighted breath. It was astonishing, exciting, so completely unexpected—like seeing a discreetly veiled woman in public, then in private lifting the veil to find a flamboyant siren behind it.

She wandered down a sweeping pathway that turned into steps beside a small, lushly planted rockery. A great Thai water jar, beautiful in its simplicity and shape and colour, stood in a bower of begonias beneath a bangalore palm.

Was Jillian right when she said Stella hadn't liked living here? But how could Stella have been bored amid so much beauty?

Minerva was admiring the amazing blue throat of a bromeliad flower when she sensed she was not alone. Her head came up swiftly. Nick was standing in the shade of the big, sweeping native trees that sheltered the hidden pool and its subtropical gardens. Sunlight dappling through the swooping branches and crinkled emerald leaves of a magnificent *puriri* set golden fire blazing around his head, but his face was in shadow. Nevertheless, Minerva could feel the cutting intensity of his gaze on her.

Her heart shook. For a stupid moment she thought there was something sinister about the way he stood there just watching her, then he walked out into the sunlight with a lithe, unconsciously graceful panther stride, and she told herself firmly not to be silly.

'This is an amazing garden,' she said as he came up, conscious that her voice was a little too high.

He looked around. 'It's my mother's favourite area. She loves exotics. She's having a great time in Singapore growing real tropicals. That's a frangipani over by the poolhouse, and the tree that looks vaguely like a jacaranda is a *tipuana*, probably better known as rosewood. It has yellow flowers.'

'You obviously don't get frosts.'

'Not many. None in this particular spot.'

Pretending to be absorbed in the garden when every sense was focused on the man who stood beside her, Minerva gazed around. A subtle male fragrance tugged mercilessly at subliminal receptors, triggering a wild, involuntary response in her.

Only once before had this unnatural awareness bedevilled her, when she had been seduced with style and not a shred of conscience by Paul. It had been the most humiliating experience of her life, and she certainly wasn't going to yield to that runaway, feverish madness again.

Stella, she thought, using the name like a talisman; this was what Stella must have felt when she saw Nick. Jealousy, hot and bright, burned evilly through her.

Clearing her throat, she managed to assume a calm, impersonal tone. 'How did your meeting go?'

'Very well.' He bent down to pull out a weed from the moist, warm soil.

As Minerva watched the easy flexion of muscles, the smooth litheness of his movements, some hitherto inviolate barrier deliquesced deep inside, unfolded a bud of desire that sent shudders of recognition through her. Why did she have to choose dangerous men to want?

'Are you on many committees?' she asked vaguely.

'Too many.' He tossed the weed on to the lawn. 'But this one I enjoy. It's an organisation that helps young farmers through the maze of acquiring their first farms.'

Was this what Jillian had referred to? Did he know that people tried to use him?

Minerva looked up into the hard, angular face above her; he was gazing up at the cliffs of the Spanish Castle, the stark, formidable line of his profile sending an eerie little shimmer of sensation through her. Yes, he had to know; the rich were often at risk. Most rapidly developed a compensatory toughness in order to deal with attempts to exploit them. She recognised it in Nick.

Not that ruthlessness excluded compassion. Hadn't he gone out into the rain to get Frank? For all his understanding of the pain the stockman was enduring, however, she sensed that Nick's forbearance would only go so far.

She said slowly, 'I didn't know the farming industry had committees like that. In fact, I thought primary producers were pretty demoralised. The last time I was home farming seemed to be going downhill fast.'

'It's recovering. The country will soon be on its feet again. Farmers first, the whole country next.'

'Doesn't it worry you that your whole livelihood is so dependent on such chancy overseas markets?'

Except that his wasn't, she recalled too late. He had his software business to cushion any fall in produce prices.

He said, 'People have to eat, and New Zealand farmers are among the best in the world. I have other strings to my bow, but even so, I've never lost faith in the hard work and adaptability of the New Zealand primary producer.'

'You seem to have a lot of trees on the property,' she said. Farming was a far safer subject than anything clsc that came to mind. While she was talking about trees she was almost able to ignore the slow, subliminal pulse of desire that throbbed through her. 'Far more than you need for shelter, surely? It looks as though nearly half the land is covered with woodlots, and that doesn't include the gullies.'

'My father fenced off the gullies so the native bush could regenerate,' he told her. 'Volcanic soil erodes very easily in our heavy rain, and he realised that the only thing that would keep the gullies intact was bush. He was one of the first landowners to become interested in farm forestry. He planted black wattle and *pinus radiatia* and eucalypts out in the paddocks, first as an experiment, then, when he realised it would work, with a kind of missionary fervour. When I took over ten years ago I added *cupressus lusitanica* and black walnuts, as well as the macrocarpa plantation.'

'Doesn't that much land in trees cut down on the number of stock you graze?'

'To a certain extent, but when the trees are eighteen months old sheep can be run under them. Cattle have to wait until the trees are five or six years old.'

She nodded. 'How about deer? I thought they were the latest fashion.'

'We're too close to the bush; if any got into the forest park they'd do untold damage. Deer don't go with trees.'

It was impossible to see any paddocks from this part of the garden; the thick remnant of native bush sheltered the garden too well. Nevertheless, Minerva kept her gaze firmly fixed in the direction of the gate, her mind equally firmly concentrated on the subject. 'What's the reason for all the trees?'

He smiled. 'The world needs paper and wood as well as food. Macrocarpa timber doesn't need preservative like pine, so it helps cut down on the use of chemicals. And trees pump oxygen into the atmosphere, and could well help the ozone layer from depleting even further. What colour are your eyes?'

Her lashes flew up. She looked straight up into a gaze as glittering and depthless as a star. And like a star his regard revealed nothing but reflected light.

He was watching her with that twisted smile. 'The oldest trick in the book,' he said calmly. 'I knew they were blue all the time.'

Swallowing to ease a suddenly parched mouth and throat, she muttered inanely, 'No. I mean yes. They're blue.'

'The colour of midnight,' he said. 'In summer, when the sky is clear.'

Midnight and stars.

No.

It was *not* going to happen again. For six years she had avoided situations like this. Never again was she going to find herself in a position where desire fought a losing struggle with will and decency and common sense.

Humiliated by her weakness and shamed by her stupidity, the nineteen-year-old Minerva had gathered what tatters of dignity were left to her and decided never to let herself get tangled up with a man who still wanted another woman.

The whole sordid episode still made her squirm. She didn't trust men who walked with the easy confidence of their male magnetism, predators whose prowling hunger turned the world into a jungle. But when Nick looked at her, when he came into the room, whenever she thought of him asleep in the bedroom next to hers, she was unable to leash the swift, silent shiver of something perilously close to anticipation.

'I thought the colour of midnight was black,' she said brusquely, trying to sound like her usual practical self.

'No, it's a blue so dark and so deep you can lose yourself in it. As distant as the outer reaches of space, as dense and intense as the sea beneath a tropical sky. A rare, exquisite colour.'

His voice struck an unknown chord deep inside her, softening her moral fibre, reducing her automatic resistance to a desperate scramble to control her unbidden, consuming reactions.

Each word was a lure, summoning the forbidden wildness from its lair inside her. Abruptly, she said, 'It sounds very pretty, but it doesn't really mean much.'

He laughed, a sudden, open outburst of amusement. It was the first time she had heard him laugh, and she was appalled at the pleasure it gave her.

'Perhaps it doesn't mean much to you,' he said, eyes gleaming through the silky fringe of his lashes. 'But you have superb eyes, as I'm sure you've been told.'

'Occasionally,' she said crisply. 'So have you. So did Stella. It must run in the family. I'd better get back; it's time to get dinner ready.'

Apparently not at all affected by her panicky reference to his dead wife, he said coolly, 'I'll come with you.'

They ate dinner together again, after which he went back to his office and drafted out letters, or whatever it was he did there. Perhaps he dreamed up new software. Minerva could only be thankful that his work kept him too busy to stay with her while she tried to read.

Eventually she gave up and went to bed, but this time, to her anguished frustration, she didn't settle down until he came up. Telling her reluctant, wilful body that she didn't want him, Minerva lay rigidly in her bed and called on all the tricks she had learned to summon sleep, but neither counting sheep nor silently chanting a mantra nor anything in between helped. Nick's image burned like wildfire behind her eyelids, the sound of his voice drowned out her thoughts, her willpower.

He blazed with the primitive appeal of dominant man, a primary, elemental attraction which had nothing to do with his dangerous, caged good looks. Apparently she was fated to fall in lust with men who somehow set free the silent, seething restlessness she had fought all her life to conquer.

She was now six years older than when she had had her heart and pride savaged by Paul. This time she was determined to deal with the situation in a vastly more adult fashion.

Nick knew, of course. Men always did. And probably, like most men, he would be quite happy to indulge himself with an affair. Stella had been dead a year; even if he mourned her sincerely, he'd be ready for some diversion now.

But that diversion was not going to be Stella's sister, even though she was stupid enough to lie in her bed and ache with a need that was as mindless as it was powerful.

After making a conscious decision to ignore Jillian's gossip, and another one not to let Nick's primeval sexuality affect her, Minerva set herself to getting as much ready as she could before the date of the dinner.

Helen Borrows rang through and said that although everything was all right, she wanted to stay with her daughter for at least another week, as the baby was not well. She hated asking, she said, but would it be all right with Minerva?

'Of course,' Minerva said instantly.

When Nick came in that evening she told him about the call. 'You don't have to stay after the dinner,' he said. 'I can look after myself. When are Ruth and Brian coming home?'

She hadn't intended to stay, but her dismissal hurt. A good reason for getting out of Spanish Castle as fast as she could. 'In three or four days, I think.'

The pale fire of his glance flashed across the resolutely impersonal countenance she turned to him. Unbidden, the tormenting flicker of awareness leapt into life.

He sensed the barriers, she thought with a tiny thrill, and for a moment his male pride wanted to test them. She saw the second he decided it wasn't worth it, and, although she was relieved, she suffered a humiliating whip of rejection that almost clawed through her outer layers of poise.

'You are very kind,' he said formally.

She shrugged. 'I'm not. I'd be a complete louse if I took off and left you without a cook, wouldn't I? Besides,' she said deliberately, 'you're family.'

Something moved in his eyes, although his handsome face revealed nothing. 'So I am,' he said with polite, alienating calmness. 'Would you do this for any member of your family, Minerva?'

'Yes.' She didn't like the faint intonation in his voice, but as long as the conversation scooted along the surface like this she was prepared to endure it.

'Your family is important to you.' It was a statement, not a question.

'Very.'

'Yet you spend most of your life away from them.'

She frowned. 'What's that got to do with anything?'

'Nothing, I suppose.' Eyes never leaving her face, he said, 'Your father was a widower when he met Ruth, wasn't he?'

'Yes. My mother was an invalid for four or five years before she died. When he met Ruth three years after that she'd just divorced her first husband.' She smiled reminiscently. 'I was ten and Stella was eleven. Both parents were worried in case we hated each other, but we surprised everyone by getting on very well together. Stella was a bit aloof with Dad, but eventually she got over that. And I adored Ruth. Well, who could help it? She loved me so much it was impossible not to reciprocate.'

'She has a great capacity for loving,' he said.

Minerva wondered exactly what he was thinking. 'What about your family?' she asked.

'The usual complement of parents,' he said evenly. 'My father died when I was twenty-four, and my mother stayed on here for a couple of years until she remarried. She's very happy with her new husband. I see her at least twice a year.'

'Did you want to come back to Spanish Castle after your father died?'

His wide shoulders moved a fraction. 'No,' he said almost indifferently, 'but tradition is a powerful force to fight and I wasn't helped by the fact that I love the place.'

'Do you ever regret it?' It was only afterwards that she realised how intimate the question was, and was astonished that he answered it so frankly.

His expression hardened. Minerva expected to be rebuffed, but he said, 'Yes. Stella found it too isolated. Sometimes I wonder whether it would have made any difference if we'd lived closer to Auckland.'

She said raggedly, 'It's useless wondering, but we can't help it. If only she'd told someone, got help! She hurt so many people—poor Ruth is slowly being eaten up with guilt. If she can't convince herself that it wasn't her fault she might never get over it.'

'I know.' His voice was level, unfaltering. 'I thought Stella might have written to you.'

'No. I wish she had.' She bit her lip, but she had to ask. 'Did she give no indication at all, Nick? Ruth said there was nothing, but—I can't see how she could have just gone temporarily mad. She must have shown some signs.'

He said steadily, 'She gave no indications at all that she might commit suicide. None.'

The night was too warm to make a fire really necessary, but Minerva had lit it because after two years spent on board a yacht a fire was a delicious luxury. It hissed quietly now, then spat out a series of sparks.

Nick's lashes were lowered against the sudden little flare, so for once she was able to scan his face. The hard-etched angles and straight lines were sharpened by the flicker of firelight. She hadn't missed the evasion in his answer, but her swift glance told her it was no use asking any further questions. He had retreated behind the barricades.

'If you get up early tomorrow,' he said without opening his eyes, 'I'll take you across to the *kauri* trees in the reserve.'

'Are those the ones you can see from the deck?'

'Yes. You can't leave Northland without admiring them, and although ours aren't as big as the ones on the West Coast they'll give you some idea of their size.'

She opened her mouth to refuse politely, then changed her mind. A visit to the *kauri* trees was not going to lead to the sort of irresponsible behaviour she was so afraid she might repeat.

Slowly, she said, 'Yes, OK. What time?'

'Six-thirty.' He opened his eyes and turned his head so she could see the one-sided quirk to his mouth. 'It'll be all right, I won't expect you to talk for at least an hour. Wear warm clothes and boots,' he said gravely, and got to his feet with the smooth ease of the predator he was. 'Goodnight.'

Minerva sat until the fire died down and the warmth faded, and in her heart there burgeoned a warmth that had nothing to do with the fire and everything to do with that ironic smile.

CHAPTER FOUR

THE *kauri* trees were amazing, their massive, grey trunks rising above the forest floor like ancient, time-flecked columns.

'I wanted to bring you at this time of the morning because—yes,' Nick said softly, 'there they are.'

The most exquisite song echoed through the trees, pure, bell-resounding notes ranging from crystalline to golden. Minerva stood as still as the man beside her, listening with a joy that was tinged with awe while the birds went through their early morning carillon.

'I've never heard them before. What are they?' she asked on a sigh when the last notes died away into the damp, echoing air.

'*Kokako*. There's a pair nesting somewhere around here.'

Although she knew the birds nested far above the ground, she gazed hopefully upwards. 'I thought they were almost extinct.'

'Not quite.' He spoke grimly. 'But they soon will be if we don't find some way of stopping possums from ravaging the bush.'

Although Minerva had spent most of the last five years overseas, she knew the damage the cute, furry little creatures, mistakenly introduced from Australia over a century ago and now no longer culled for their fur, were doing to New Zealand's precious forest cover.

'We can get closer to the *kauris*,' Nick said. 'The department of conservation's put in a boardwalk here so that the trunks and roots aren't damaged.'

Their path took them diagonally across a sloping hillside to a valley. The bushy crowns of more *kauris* rose through the rapidly thinning mist, and as it dissi-

69

pated the trunks, massive, elemental, their solidity varied by patches of soft pink and amber where bark had flaked free, came into sight.

A sudden piercing emotion stabbed Minerva's heart. At that moment she was happier than she had ever been before. Don't be an idiot, she warned herself as she stumbled.

Instantly Nick caught her arm and held her until she regained stability. Awareness, fierce and unrestrained, fired every cell in her body.

'Thanks,' she muttered, carefully pulling away.

The boardwalk opened out into a viewing platform. There, over a valley of treeferns where tiny fantails flitted and cheeped and ate greedily of the insects they disturbed, Minerva was able to look around and see a circle of *kauri* trees, set apart as carefully as though some race of humans in the dawn of time had planted them to make a temple to unknown gods. This was what it must have been like when the world began.

Apart from the songs of the birds and a stream somewhere in the misty distance, the only sounds she could hear were her own breathing and the rapid thud of her heart.

Seemingly content to remain silent, Nick stood beside her and looked out across the ferny floor of the little valley, his lean hands gripping the railings. Minerva dragged her gaze away from those hands, banished the vagrant images they conjured, of them on her white skin, caressing . . .

'*Kauris* are really something,' she said quietly, in a voice that barely trembled. 'I've seen taller trees, and older trees, and trees that are more beautiful, but I've never seen trees as awe-inspiring. They make me wish I was the first person to set foot on New Zealand a thousand years ago and see it as it had been since the beginning of time, untouched by humans.'

'To set foot in unknown lands,' he said, some of her own awe and impossible longing reflected in his deep voice.

Although it was dangerously seductive to find that they shared emotions and outlook, she had to be ruthless. There was no future for this sudden, tumultuous attraction. Pride, common sense, the tangled circumstances, Nick's own armour of coldness, dictated that she refuse to allow her stupid emotions any rein at all. Her experience with Paul had taught her how important self-respect was. A small amount of suffering now meant avoiding a greater pain later.

If she surrendered to the treacherous instincts that throbbed through her, she'd end up with a broken heart instead of one that was merely cracked.

But—until they left this place, she'd savour the timeless magic of the moment.

At last Nick looked at his watch and said reluctantly, 'We have to go.'

Back in the car both remained silent. Minerva looked distantly at the now repaired signpost, and wondered whether she would have gone on if she had known what lay ahead.

No, of course not. She wasn't stupid. She'd have turned tail and fled all the way back to Auckland, not stopping until she got on a plane for the Virgin Islands. Nobody went *looking* for heartbreak.

'One day,' he said casually, as though promising a treat to a child, 'we'll see the dawn rise from the top of the Spanish Castle. It's well worth getting up in the dark.'

'I'm sure it is.' But she was withdrawing, girding herself for the battle with her weakness, and her voice reflected her retreat.

A sharp glance from eyes as silver as the sea beneath a dawn sun sent shivers of sensation rippling through her.

Minerva couldn't imagine Nick so lost in the throes of love that he married a woman he had known only for

a month. Yet Stella had broken through seemingly
without any effort at all.

Shamingly, for the first time since adolescence Minerva
found herself wishing that she was more than just pre-
sentable. A slim, boyish figure and a face that, apart
from eyes and good skin, had little to recommend it,
didn't make for the sort of sexy provocation that attracted men.

Melancholy condensed deep inside her, bringing with
it a greyness that all the logic in the world wouldn't
banish. She had never been one to build Spanish castles
in her own personal life, to waste time and mental energy
in useless longing for the hopelessly unattainable, but
this fierce physical enslavement was shatteringly difficult to cope with; it sent her defences flying.

Well, she thought acidly, she'd just have to put up
with it until it went away. She had recovered from Paul
Penn's assassination attempt on her self-respect; she'd
get over this entirely inappropriate reaction to her sister's widower.

The two days that followed were oddly serene. Spring
moved inexorably through its paces while Minerva organised the dinner with all the skill at her command. It
was the only thing she could give Nick. Ironic that she,
a career woman with a stimulating future all planned,
should only be able to show her feelings in the traditional woman's way!

Nick was out the night before the dinner. Minerva went
to bed early, glad of the respite even though she wondered jealously just where he'd gone. Genevieve
Chatswood's place, perhaps. The very uncompromising
Ms Chatswood had rung a couple of times, and been
affable but distant to Minerva.

Once Jillian had answered, took a message and banged
the receiver down, her scowl revealing exactly what she
thought of the other woman. Minerva had cut her off
when she began to mutter about stuck-up bitches who
were totally in love with themselves, but she found herself

silently agreeing. At least she was spared Genevieve's presence at the dinner; her last call had been to tell Nick that she had to go to Auckland on Saturday morning to meet the Japanese importer of her orchids.

Minerva bitterly resented the fact that she was relieved. She hated this. It hurt. She hated the jealousy, hated the despair and loneliness that seared through her when she thought of any other woman in Nick's arms. She hated not being able to go to sleep until he came home.

Above all, she hated not being able to control her emotions.

And she wasn't going to be able to do anything about it until she left Nick and Spanish Castle far behind: just hang on, one day at a time, and hope for the best.

The car purred in around two in the morning. Gritty-eyed, Minerva exhaled a sigh of relief and turned over. Now at last she could get to sleep.

Her lids were already heavy when Nick's soft footsteps stopped outside her room. He said her name quietly. If she'd been asleep she wouldn't have heard him.

Minerva was out of bed and opening the door before she had time to consider whether she was doing the right thing. Horrified, she glanced from his face to the blood-stained towel wrapped around his right hand.

'I can't bandage it myself,' he said collectedly. 'There's a medicine kit in my bathroom; can you do it for me?'

'Yes, of course.' Shrugging into her dressing-gown, she belted it tightly as she went with him into his room.

He sat down on the chair in the corner of the big bathroom and let her unwrap his hand. Minerva's breath whistled between her teeth when she saw the jagged scratches and teeth marks across the palm and wrist of his right hand. One had missed the blue veins in his wrist by a bare centimetre.

'What happened?' she asked jerkily, tipping disinfectant into the handbasin and turning on the taps.

'I had to kill a possum.' He leaned back and watched as she reached for a clean hand towel.

'With your bare hands? It'll be better to soak it first. Surely a possum didn't do all that damage?'

Although the lacerations must have stung he didn't wince, not even the instant the water closed over the scratches. The silver eyes were fixed on her face. She was close enough to smell a faint odour of brandy on his breath.

'They've got teeth and claws. When it comes to fighting for their lives it's surprising the havoc they can create. I used a tyre jack,' he said evenly. 'Someone had run the possum over then driven on without making sure it was dead.'

His voice didn't alter but Minerva looked up. The cold disgust in his expression made her shiver. 'OK, that should have done it,' she said.

He took his hand out of the water. Carefully, she began to dry the cuts.

'It had internal injuries and a couple of broken legs. I thought one blow would do the job,' he went on unhurriedly, 'but possums are damned hard to kill, and one wasn't enough. It played possum. When I picked it up to throw it off the road it defended itself the only way it knew how. So I had to keep on hitting it until I finally managed to kill it.'

'Not much fun,' Minerva said gently.

He closed his eyes. 'Not a lot. A quick, clean death is one thing. This was brutal and ugly.'

None of the bites or scratches was particularly deep but they looked nasty. Frowning, Minerva said, 'Shouldn't you have a jab for this?'

'There's some antibiotic ointment in the first-aid kit. It will do.'

She found it and smeared it on, then bandaged the hand. 'I think you should go to the doctor first thing in the morning,' she told him mildly. 'I'll drive you down.'

He frowned. 'Don't fuss,' he said, but there was a thread of metal in his tone.

Unintimidated, she lifted her brows. 'I'm not fussing. Animal bites are dangerous; they're inclined to infect. You'd be silly not to do something about it.'

He smiled, the lop-sided charm very evident. Minerva was abruptly conscious that her dressing-gown was thin cotton, and that beneath it she wore nothing but an even thinner nightgown.

'All right,' he said wearily as she began to clean up. 'It'll have to be early, though; I've a lot to do tomorrow.'

Dropping the hand towel into the basket, she nodded. 'I'll see you in the morning.'

He rose, dwarfing her. 'Just one thing,' he said. 'Can you undo my cufflinks? I can manage the buttons, but the links are a bit tricky.'

For a second she froze. Then she said, 'Yes, of course,' managing to make her voice steady and obliging, nothing more.

Miraculously she didn't fumble, even though her breath came short and fast through her lips, dragged into lungs suddenly starved of air. The hint of brandy on his breath was blended into the male scent she found so stimulating; her nerves jumped as her deft fingers worked the cuffs free.

'There,' she said, stepping back, her voice resolutely impersonal. 'Goodnight. I'll see you in the morning.'

'Goodnight.' He smiled at her, his stern mouth softening, his eyes translucent beneath the thick lashes. 'Thank you, Minerva. For listening, as well as the Florence Nightingale stuff.'

The kiss was light, almost tentative. Afterwards Minerva was sure that if it hadn't caught her so unawares she wouldn't have reacted with such surprise, allowing herself to sink into the sensation of his lips against hers with never a moment of sober logic. And if she hadn't done that, the kiss might have stayed as simple, as *friendly* as it had begun.

But she *was* taken by surprise. That gentle touch sent skyrockets soaring unharnessed through her body. And when he felt her momentary surrender, the subtle yielding of woman to man, the predator in him took over and the kiss changed into something very different, dark and primitive and masterful, a claiming that smashed with elemental force through barricades set up by fear and experience and took her over completely.

It lasted forever; it didn't last long enough. When it ended Minerva couldn't call back the muffled protest that slipped free.

'Damn,' he said in a voice that found an echo in her soul. 'Damn it all to *hell*. I've been trying to avoid this ever since I saw you...'

His mouth was a fraction of a centimetre above hers. Dazedly, Minerva looked up into eyes where an icy storm roared out of control, an untamed tempest that matched the hurricane raging inside her.

She had just enough will-power to pull away.

But as she moved he muttered, 'No,' and his mouth came down again, coaxing hers open in a kiss so deep and intimate that it leached the strength from her bones.

Her brain was screaming, This is not possible! even as she sagged against him, that final spark of resistance overshadowed by an infinitely greater conflagration.

The aroused hunger of his body transmitted its own particular spell. Minerva's arms slid around his shoulders; slow and seductive as a cat, she arched against him, inciting him with small, barely perceptible movements of her body, whipping up an appetite that had been smouldering for too long.

'Bloody hell,' he muttered, his voice harsh and shaking, guttural with emotion.

She had wondered what he would be like when he slipped the leash he kept over his emotions; now she knew. Fierce and demanding, he made no bones about what he wanted.

And what he wanted was her complete capitulation. She shuddered to the need vibrating through his lean body, the white-hot hunger that arced between them when his mouth discovered the tender spot behind her ear, the unexpected *frisson* that shook her as he bit tenderly along her jawbone.

He was all male, strong and arrogant in his demands, yet he touched her with a totally unexpected gentleness. His hand at her breast made her flinch, but the swift, involuntary reaction was superseded by a flood of honeyed fire that spread through her from the fork of her body.

When his thumb rasped across the proud aureole of her nipple, Minerva said something in an anguished voice.

And he almost flung her across the room.

She cried out, grabbing the back of the chair in time to save herself from ending up a crumpled heap on the floor. Her breath lifted her chest, rasping painfully into her lungs.

Eyes flat and lethal beneath half-closed lids, he looked at her with a sudden, deadly antagonism, the harsh, unyielding angles of his face chiselled into complete rejection.

Then he turned away, standing with hands clenched on the marble vanity unit, his proud head bowed as he fought for control.

'Get—the—hell—out—of—here.' The words were ground out, a stark, vibrating pause between each one.

In the mirror Minerva could see his utter determination. Wrenching her gaze away, she found it lingering compulsively on the corded muscles in his shoulders. With the back of her hand pressed to her mouth, she turned and fled.

What followed was the longest night Minerva had ever spent. Humiliation ate into her soul while chaotic fragments of memory and thoughts tossed around her brain.

At last, some time towards dawn, she decided militantly that she would not allow Nick Peveril to do this to her. She knew damned well he was attracted to her; he had made the first move. It was not her fault that he had then changed his mind and rebuffed her callously and cruelly. The shame and embarrassment were not hers. Tomorrow she would hold her head high.

It was easy enough to make the decision to preserve her self-esteem; it was a lot harder to face him over the breakfast table with a bland, impassive face and eyes from which all trace of speculation had gone.

After one penetrating glance he said in a level, unhurried voice, 'I'm sorry I was so brutal last night.'

Not trusting herself to speak with any degree of composure, Minerva shrugged.

He frowned, but went on coolly, 'I lost control. If I hadn't managed to put a stop to it we'd have ended up in bed together.'

There must have been several ways of telling him she didn't want to hear his excuses, but her mind went blank and the muscles in her larynx refused to obey her.

'And,' he went on remorsefully, 'I assume that you're just as opposed to that as I am.'

This time she managed to speak. 'I am,' she returned, her voice as brittle and remote as an iceberg.

If he said anything about being friends—but no, he wouldn't.

He didn't. He was an experienced man, sophisticated enough to know that once two people had kissed, had been singed by the merciless fires of passion, there was no going back. They were now aware of each other in a fundamental way that could no longer be ignored.

'When this dinner is over,' he said abruptly, 'you must feel free to go.'

'Yes.' Minerva cast about for something to disguise the bare monosyllable, but nothing came.

He waited courteously, then said, 'I can look after myself.'

'Helen——'

His brows lifted. In a voice that would have frozen water in the tropics he said, 'There's no need to call her back until she feels happy about coming.'

At least the housekeeper was a neutral subject. 'Have you heard from her again?'

'She rang a few minutes ago. Her daughter's fine, and the baby has the all-clear now, but naturally she wants to stay a little longer to satisfy herself that they can manage.'

'Of course. How is your hand?'

Such stilted words. They had never, not even in the first days, spoken with such care, such need to hide their feelings. In spite of the emotions that were clawing her heart Minerva kept her face carefully immobile.

'It's fine. I've rung the local doctor and he's sending something up on the rural delivery van for it.'

'Good.' She chewed a piece of toast and pretended to be thinking deeply about the day ahead.

'Have you everything you need?' he asked.

'Yes, it's all under control.'

All that day the previous night's fiasco lingered at the back of her mind like a bruise on her consciousness. Fortunately, she was so busy with preparations for the dinner that she had neither the time nor the opportunity to brood.

Jillian, too, was at full stretch. She spent the morning cleaning and polishing, then after lunch carefully and with due ceremony damped down and ironed the huge damask tablecloth. She and Minerva spread it over the protective undercloth, then, while Minerva arranged the flowers, Jillian disappeared to iron its thirty napkins.

'They lived well when these were made,' she said when she returned with them. She looked down the table, her gaze kindling with pleasure. 'Hey, that looks terrific. You've got a good eye for decorations.'

Minerva had wound a trail of miniature arum lilies, yellow spray carnations and loquat leaves down the centre of the table, the soft little flowers of the carnations contrasting with the more sculptural forms of the lilies and the thick, stiff leaves. White candles in bronzed glass candlesticks picked up bronze tints from the foliage, and gave an airy splendour to the setting of china, white and gold and green, an old-fashioned design that might have been made for the superb room.

Perhaps it had been.

'You've done a better job than Helen Borrows,' Jillian said as she arranged the napkins. 'She's OK, but she hasn't got much imagination. Pretty posies, that's her style. Well, I'll be off. I'll come back at six, but don't you leave me in the kitchen on my own all night. I'm going to need someone to hold my hand occasionally.'

'Don't worry, I'll slip away as often as I can. Anyway, you can cope.'

Jillian's sharp face flushed. Being Jillian, she accepted the praise without comment. 'Who's coming with the Brazilians?'

'The local MP, a cabinet minister and somebody from the trade commission.'

'Oh, high-powered stuff. How can you be so calm? Helen would be in a real tizz by now. Still, you've cooked for real celebrities, so I suppose it's all in a day's work for you.'

Minerva gave her a somewhat abstracted smile. 'I still get nervous. I'm just good at hiding it,' she said, not quite truthfully.

Jillian grinned. 'Well, if the food's half as good as the table, those Brazilians won't know what's hit them.'

Twitching a leaf into place, Minerva stood back. The meal was as ready as it could be at this stage, the house was gleaming, sweet with beeswax and lavender and flowers, the gardens glowed in their full spring beauty. She had spoken to the two high-school boys who were acting as waiters, and was confident they knew their job.

With nothing more to do, she went into the kitchen and made herself a pot of tea, resolutely pushing back recalcitrant memories while she checked off her list. The roasted salmon was cold, the tuna waiting to be sliced, the lamb and venison under control, as were the soup and the pudding.

All she had to do was drink her tea, shower, rest for half an hour, then dress. It would be the first time she had actually cooked a meal and acted as hostess at the same time, and until yesterday she had been a little nervous.

One thing last night had done, she thought with a sardonic smile, was wipe those fears from her mind.

Six hours later she was exhausted yet triumphant. It had been one of those magical occasions that the guests would remember with nothing but pleasure. The food had been magnificent, the company superb; Jillian had worked like a Trojan in the kitchen, and the two high-school boys had behaved impeccably, apart from a few nervous guffaws behind the scenes. Minerva had received so many dark-eyed, smiling compliments that she was a trifle giddy with it all.

It was midnight before the last one left. When the red tail-lights had disappeared behind the screening trees Minerva turned to Nick, saturnine in black and white evening clothes, and said, 'I'll just hop into the kitchen——'

'No,' he said curtly, watching her with narrowed gaze. 'Get up to bed.'

She bit her lip, but obeyed. All through the evening she'd been kept on edge by the need to seem perfectly at ease, yet not to presume, so that no one would make the wrong assumptions about their relationship. Acutely conscious of Nick being the perfect host, she had become even more conscious of disturbing vibrations from him as the South American guests bent over her hand and paid her court.

'All right,' she said and took a couple of steps up the stairs.

'Minerva,' he said from the foot of the staircase.

She turned her head, met the icy fire of his eyes straight on. Clutched by the first intimation of desire, the base of her spine dissolved. 'Yes?'

'Thank you.' He looked saturnine, very much a fallen angel, all pride and arrogance.

She managed to produce a smile. 'It was nothing. Glad I could help,' she said negligently, her heart beating rapidly in her throat at his slow, intent, concentrated survey.

Perhaps it was that which made her clumsy enough to stumble. Nick closed the distance between them so swiftly that she hadn't reached the floor before she was pulled into his warm, strong grasp.

Harshly he said, 'You're barely able to stand,' and lifted her, carrying her up the staircase and into her room.

'Nick,' she said in a high, constricted voice. 'Put me down.'

He did, depositing her rather more forcefully than she liked on the bed, then bent to ease her shoes from her feet.

She said in stifled tones, 'I can do that.'

'Of course you can.' His fingers moved over the fine bones of her feet in a slow, rhythmical movement. 'Your muscles are as knotted as hell.'

Minerva almost purred with pleasure, but the absorbed look on his face was a threat she had no intention of ignoring. 'A bath will fix that,' she said, trying to sound brisk and competent and fully in charge.

Sit up! she commanded fiercely. Sit up and tell him to go away. But her bones had melted and wouldn't obey her. She lay like some languid, obedient captive, prey to passion, while his skilful, erotic massage moved to her tense calves.

She looked helplessly at his bent head, noting the soft golden strands amid the rich amber hair, the way it waved close to his splendid head. Her body sprang to insistent, vibrant life.

Shakily, thinly, she whispered, 'Nick, please go.'

'Do you want me to?' he asked beneath his breath.

He pinned her with a glance, sharp as a crystal lance, savagely possessive. It had been that possessiveness that had sizzled through the air all night. Oh, it hadn't been overt; she doubted whether anyone else had noticed it, but she had felt the focus of his attention even when he wasn't looking at her.

She touched her tongue to lips that were suddenly dry. 'I—please, Nick...'

'I've imagined you saying that to me so many times,' he said conversationally, straightening. His gaze, glittering with unhidden passion, roamed the length of her body, the heart-shaped contours of her face, as though she had been chosen for him, carried ceremoniously in and left lying on his bed like some primitive sacrifice to his virility. He yanked his tie loose.

'So many times,' he said, and knelt to kiss her, his words slow and heavy and deep against her lips, 'and in so many different ways. Pleadingly, and commandingly, and hopefully, and easily, and always I say yes, yes, yes, I will, Minerva, lovely Minerva with eyes deep enough to lose my soul in and tempting red lips and skin so white that my hands look barbaric against it. I want to make you mine, to take it all, your sleek, slim, white naiad's body, your forthrightness and your competence, but mostly your honesty and your open, frank response——'

Responding without restraint to the naked need, the aggressive hunger that should have terrified the life out of her and didn't, she stopped his words with her mouth.

By the time the kiss ended he was beside her on the bed, one lean leg over hers, and they were pressed together, heart thudding into heart, hips melded, all pretence at control burnt away like morning mist before the full heat of the sun.

'Minerva,' he said, pulling the little black dress down, over her arms, down to her waist.

She was so bemused that she let him. But when the sudden cool air dissipated some of the heated fumes of desire and she would have hidden her inadequate breasts from him, he pulled her arms away and held them pinioned in his lean, strong fingers on the pillow above her head so that she was exposed to him.

Minerva closed her eyes, but she still felt his scrutiny, shivered in the heat of his gaze on the soft white globes. When she lifted her lashes again he was still looking at her with the ardent hunger of a man about to arrive at the end of his rainbow, reach his Spanish castle, his long-desired, unattainable aim.

Lowering his head, he kissed each tight little aureole, telling her in his deep, slurred voice just how beautiful they were to him. The touch of his mouth filled her with unbelievable sweetness and need, so that she quivered, her eyes frantic beneath the heavy fringe of her lashes as she tried to break free of his grip and open the front of his shirt.

But he kept her manacled, smiling his satisfaction against her skin. 'No,' he said, taking a supplicant little nipple into the heated moisture of his mouth.

Minerva's body arched into a taut bow. His hand slid down, found the sensitive skin of her thigh, then efficiently stripped her satin knickers from her body. In some forgotten corner of her mind Minerva realised that this was going too far, that she should stop him, but the violent enchantment summoned by his mouth banished all logic, drowned her will-power.

His hand returned to the juncture of her thighs. Cupping the soft mound there, he pressed rhythmically. Arrows of delight flashed through her. She moaned his name, and he laughed.

'Yes,' he said thickly, 'I thought you'd like that.'

Dimly she was aware that although she was shooting out of control, his desire was still leashed by the force of his will, but by then it was too late for resistance. Minerva sobbed with frustration as his maddening mouth roved her breasts, discovered the indents of her waist, the narrow hollow of her hip, the taut curve of her stomach.

His hand moved, an exploratory finger testing, measuring the depth, while another smoothed gently around the small source of all her passion. A shattering, heart-stopping pleasure arched her body free of the bed. She was taken by his skilled touch into a place where nothing mattered but the waves of sensation that carried her higher and higher into a place she had never been before. Racked by ecstasy, her body convulsed, transformed into a focus of pleasure so intense that it shattered something final and fundamental inside her.

She came down quickly, slipping into lethargy, into satiation, cradled against him.

Eventually, when her heartbeat had subsided to normal, he kissed her, said, 'I'll see you in the morning,' and got up.

She levered herself up onto her elbow. 'Nick?' she said uncertainly.

He had slung his jacket over his arm. Without looking at her he said, 'We have to talk. Not now—you're too tired. And tomorrow I have to go around with this damned official party until late in the afternoon. It will have to wait until tomorrow night.'

Something cold and menacing, some ominous warning, moved sluggishly through the warm, golden repletion of a moment before. Minerva bit her lip, staring at the harsh line of his profile, his set stance.

Nodding reluctantly, she whispered. 'Yes. All right.'

While she finished undressing she tried to work out exactly what was making her so uneasy. It wasn't just that she had let him touch her so intimately; there was something else gnawing at the fragile fabric of her composure.

She looked across the room at the suggestively rumpled bed. Nick could have taken their lovemaking to its logical conclusion: she wouldn't have been able to stop him. She had been lost entirely in the spell of his sexuality, of his experience and skill.

Surely his restraint meant he wanted more from her than just a quick tumble in the hay?

Or did he despise her for her ready surrender?

She climbed into the bed, still faintly musky with his male presence, and lay with her arms behind her head, fingers linked, staring up at the sunburst pattern of silk above her. She didn't believe in love at first sight. Lust at first sight—yes, that happened. That was what had happened with Paul. Love was different; if the episode with Paul had taught her nothing, it had taught her that.

Was it love, this wild, sweet yearning, this need to give and take from Nick, to just be with him, no matter if he never loved her?

Even if it was, it was doomed. For some reason—almost certainly to do with Stella—Nick wasn't letting any woman get close to him again. Minerva didn't blame him; her barriers had crashed into place after Paul had betrayed her.

It was a sharp irony that in spite of her years of caution she had been seduced again, once more by her own weakness. She'd been so determined to conquer the initial, heated desire that she hadn't noticed when love—if that was what it was—sneaked in unseen, unheralded, a spy in the house of her heart, and undermined the walls from within.

Had it happened in the evenings when they had talked about anything and everything, and she had repressed her feverish awareness in the belief that she could form some tenuous friendship with him and still keep her integrity?

She turned over on to her stomach. It was too late to worry about how her complete surrender had happened, or when; it had happened. Now she had to find some way of dealing with it.

She lay for a while mulling over the rapturous, terrifying moments in his arms, then tumbled into a sleep so profound that she didn't wake until late.

Nick was heading towards the back door when she got downstairs. Opening her mouth to say good morning, Minerva was forestalled by Jillian's knock.

'It's only me!' she called.

Minerva stood still, her eyes locked on to Nick's remote face.

'I'll see you this evening,' he said.

The dark foreboding thickened into fear, almost eclipsing the hope that had struggled into existence some time during the night: during her dreams, probably, when the curb of consciousness was relaxed, allowing needs and desires full expression.

'All right,' Minerva said quietly. Although she knew neither her voice nor her face revealed any emotion, she noted with resignation Jillian's eyes swivel from one to the other with an alert, almost avid interest.

So Minerva wasn't surprised at morning tea time when Jillian said with an air of casual interest that didn't fool her for a moment, 'You and Nick seem to be getting on better now.'

'We've always got on well,' Minerva returned tranquilly.

Jillian directed a sceptical look at her. 'Oh, really? I thought things were pretty sticky at first.'

'Hardly. We were just strangers.'

The other woman didn't sniff, but her expression indicated she'd like to. 'If he was my brother-in-law I'd never look at him without remembering what he did to my sister,' she said acidly.

Minerva stifled a quick, tart reply. This was her own fault. If she didn't want to hear gossip she should have made it clear from the first. Mildly, she returned, 'But that's none of our business.'

Jillian retorted with relish, 'Just be careful, that's all. I mean, he's gorgeous, but—he's not very trustworthy.'

Some of the shimmering, glowing hope died inside Minerva. She turned away, but Jillian ploughed on, 'He left your sister here by herself while he went off on a dirty weekend with his girlfriend. That was the weekend she killed herself.'

Minerva's mouth dropped. She swung around, unable to stop the words tumbling out. 'He—what?'

Jillian looked both angry and smug. 'Oh, he kept it quiet—you can do that sort of thing when you've got money and power—but I know he was spending the weekend with Genevieve Chatswood.'

'Genevieve?'

'Yeah, stuck-up bitch. They were having a hot affair when Stella came on the scene, and I know for a fact, because I overheard her tell one of her friends right here in this house, that Genevieve would have done anything to break up the marriage. She did, in the end. They were staying together at her parents' house on Lake Rotoiti that weekend.'

Minerva felt sick, but she said carefully, 'Perhaps her parents were there, too.'

'Perhaps they were, but when Helen Borrows rang through to tell Nick his wife was dead it was my lady Genevieve who took the call, all sleepy and tired and husky-voiced, and then handed it straight to him. Very suspicious, I thought it was.'

Minerva asked curtly, 'How do you know all this?'

Flushing, Jillian lifted her chin. 'I was here; I'd come over early to see whether I could do anything. We were going to the beach with friends that day, and I wanted to ring them to say we wouldn't be coming, but when I picked up the receiver Helen Borrows was just asking Genevieve to get Nick. I couldn't put the phone down in case it clicked and they'd know someone was listening.' She looked virtuous. 'So I held it away from my ear. But if she wasn't sleeping beside him I'll eat my hat. And I'll bet your sister knew all about it, and that's why she killed herself.'

She was telling the truth, about the main events, anyway. Minerva wouldn't have put money on her not listening. 'I see,' she said tonelessly. 'But if you think that's why Stella committed suicide, why didn't you tell anyone so that it came out at the inquest?'

Jillian laughed scornfully. 'I'm not stupid. I had no proof. Nick's got a lot of power. Over us, especially. If I'd opened my mouth there'd have been a hell of a stink.'

And no chance of finance for the farm she and her husband wanted so desperately. Minerva thought she had never disliked anyone quite so much as she did at that moment. 'Why are you telling me now?' she asked remotely.

'I think you should know.' Once more Jillian managed a righteous expression. 'That day when she was crying in the car, she said, "There's nothing for me now, nothing at all. I might as well be dead". I was worried, but when I saw her the next day she seemed OK, so I didn't do anything about it.'

She drank more coffee, then said half beneath her breath, 'I keep wondering whether there was anything I could have done. But she didn't seem that upset the next day—in fact, she laughed it off, and said it was just the time of the month.'

'She was probably right,' Minerva said wearily, her dislike and anger fading at the genuine concern in the younger woman's tone. Why should she blame Jillian for looking after her own interests? 'If Stella had decided to kill herself, nothing you could have done would have made any difference. Ultimately we're all responsible for our own actions.'

'Yeah, well, if that's true I wouldn't like to be Genevieve Chatswood. Or Nick, come to think of it.' She sent Minerva another of those darting little looks. 'Although, I don't know. I mean, your sister and Nick weren't getting on all that well. Well, it stands to reason— they didn't sleep in the same room.'

Without saying anything, Minerva picked up her cup and took it across to the sink.

'I'm sorry—I shouldn't have told you, I suppose.' Jillian's tone combined alarm and contrition. 'John keeps telling me my tongue will land me in trouble if I don't watch it. But you're nice—you're not a snotty piece like the Chatswood woman, up herself. And I liked your sister.'

'It's all right,' Minerva said flatly, swirling water around in the mug. She didn't know who she despised more, Nick for having an affair and hushing it up, or herself for falling for his specious charm. All she wanted to do was run as far and as fast as possible.

Jillian clearly regretted her revelations. For the rest of the morning she kept well out of Minerva's way, and when the clock struck twelve, instead of staying for a short chat as she'd begun to do, called out, 'See you later,' as she was halfway through the door.

Minerva was grateful for her swift departure. Standing at the bench mechanically preparing lunch, she wondered just what she should do now.

So Nick had been having an affair. Still might be, for all anyone knew. Genevieve Chatswood had definitely looked at him with more than friendship. Minerva was horrified to realise that her first reaction was sheer, jealous outrage. For several furious moments she didn't even think of Stella.

But soon, too soon, the memory of her sister's pain came sharply to her mind, and she had to sit down, her hands clasped tensely before her on the table.

Had Stella committed suicide because Nick and Genevieve were lovers?

CHAPTER FIVE

Rubbing a hand across her eyes, Minerva forced herself upright. When Nick told her about Stella she would at least *know*. Then the hollow nausea in her stomach might go away.

In the window she caught a glimpse of her reflection: tragic eyes the colour of a stormy sky, soft red mouth turned down in a clown's grimace. Make it not be his fault, she thought fiercely, absurdly, and put the food away, unable to face the thought of eating.

Too soon Jillian arrived back, carrying a bundle of letters which she thrust at Minerva with an eagerness that had something unsettling about it.

'You'd better sort it,' she said, speaking so intensely that it sent a faint shiver up Minerva's spine. 'There's one for you.'

'I'll take it into the office,' Minerva said firmly, heading inside.

She had only shuffled three letters on to Nick's desk when she saw the reason for Jillian's half-terrified interest.

Ice chilled Minerva's blood. Stella's handwriting, bold and slightly scrawly, burned into her eyes. Creased and faded, the envelope had the grubby, secondhand appearance of something that had lain around in obscure places for months. Stella had sent it to the yacht; additional hands had indited a variety of instructions, until someone had got tired of sending it on and stamped in big red letters 'ADDRESS UNKNOWN; RETURN TO SENDER'.

Pressing her lips together to stop them trembling, Minerva peered at the original postmark through half-closed eyes. It was almost impossible to read, but she deciphered enough to realise that Stella had posted the letter just before she died.

Part of the reason it was hard to read, Minerva realised, was that her hand was shaking. She collapsed into a chair, staring at the letter. Panic oozed in a sickening surge through her. In that innocent-looking envelope could be the answer she wanted. Did she want it that badly?

If she screwed it up and burnt it she might never have to face just how much Nick had to do with Stella's death. She would believe anything he told her——

The colour left her face in a clammy rush. God, she was expecting him to lie! And for a moment she'd wanted to accept his lie rather than face the truth. Her cowardice sickened her, yet the temptation to do it, to scrumple the thing up and throw it into the range unopened, unread, was almost irresistible.

Setting her jaw, the muscles in her neck aching with sudden tension, she slit the envelope, holding the letter knife in one hand while she read her stepsister's last letter to her. Barely a page long, it had been scribbled two days before she died.

Darling Min, just a note. Min, I'm so miserable.

'Miserable' had been underlined three times.

Hot tears stung Minerva's eyes, an ache closed her throat. Putting down the knife, she wiped her lids with her knuckle and, swallowing fiercely, forced herself to keep reading.

I should have known that fairy-stories only belong in children's books, but I thought everything would be so wonderful. It's so unfair.

'Unfair' was underlined three times too.

It's all such an awful mess, and there's no way out. Why should I be the one to be punished for the rest of my life when it wasn't even my fault? Or perhaps he was telling the truth, and there is something wrong with me. Nothing's ever been right for me since then. It doesn't matter now, anyway. I've come to the end of my tether. I wish you were here, Min. I love you and I miss you so much.

The signature was barely legible, but there was no mistaking the childish kisses she had signed after it.

Minerva put the letter down, oddly surprised to see that her hand was perfectly steady on the polished surface of the desk. She fished for her handkerchief and blew her nose, then gave in to the sudden, wild relief that swamped her, a relief that was banished by a second reading.

For a long time she stood looking out over the smooth manicured lawn. The sad little letter made her feel wretched, but it was her capitulation before she read it that gave her the bitter taste in her mouth.

In spite of their short acquaintance, in spite of everything, she loved Nick.

It had to be love. Only love could make her prepared to sacrifice her integrity and peace of mind, ready to burn the letter and live with uncertainty for the rest of her life.

'God,' she whispered, sinking down into the chair.

She had always despised women who loved unworthy men. Perhaps it was fitting that she should fall in love with two men who—no, that was untrue. She hadn't loved Paul. That had been lust.

And Nick might not be unworthy.

Her eyes fell on the letter again. A bleak smile robbed her face of softness. Stella couldn't have been more vague if she'd tried, but it was clear that Nick had blamed her for whatever had gone wrong with their marriage.

Had her sister loved Nick like this, stupidly, desperately, transformed by the sheer force of her emotions into a different woman? The Minerva who loved him seemed a million miles removed from the Minerva Robertson who was competent and practical and ran her own life with success. Love had sapped her self-respect;

had it done that to Stella, too, until the only way she
could deal with what she had become was kill herself?

Stuffing the letter into the pocket of her apron,
Minerva ran upstairs, treading with light, quick footsteps, straining her ears like a burglar to make sure Jillian
wasn't around.

Once in her room she pushed both letter and envelope
into the drawer that held her scarves and handkerchiefs.
The sick emptiness in her stomach had been augmented
by a headache. The hours until Nick came back stretched
like infinity before her.

And what then? a malicious voice from her unconscious mocked. What will you do if he did drive Stella
to her lonely death? Leave him? Did this damned, inconvenient love have limits? Surely she couldn't love a
man who had hurt her stepsister so badly that she'd killed
herself rather than face the pain.

God help me, I don't know.

Fragments of the letter danced tauntingly in front of
her eyes. Why had Stella made it so cryptic? What had
she meant?

With unbearable slowness the afternoon crept by. Each
minute that crawled past increased her tension, until
when Nick finally arrived at six-thirty every nerve in her
body was stretched to its fullest extent. Even Penelope
was affected; instead of being in her usual place on the
stool she was crouched beneath it, watching Minerva
warily with wide, unblinking eyes.

Although Nick didn't smile when he came through the
door, his eyes searched her face with such disturbing
demand that Minerva was overwhelmed by a drenching
sweetness. A sweetness she had to ignore.

'Dinner's almost ready,' she said quietly.

He made no attempt to touch her, but the cold fire
of his gaze darkened.

'Thanks.'

During dinner he was once more the man she had met
on that first night, unreachable behind the barriers of

his self-containment. It seemed impossible that a man with such seamless, almost inhuman control could ever lose his temper.

She asked after his day.

'It went well. The Brazilians enjoyed themselves, and were very interested in some of the new breeds of cattle. Even the government party seemed happy with the programme,' he said, and with smooth, distant courtesy began to tell her of an amusing incident that had happened during the day.

Minerva pretended to be interested; it was all very polite, very distant. They progressed to discussing a film, then dissected a television programme as they finished the meal.

'All right,' he said when the dishes had been stacked into the dishwasher and the kitchen left shiny and tidy, and she was sitting on the sofa in front of the fire. 'What's the matter?'

She didn't look at him. The fire crackled and spat. She felt the cushions of the sofa give as he sat down beside her.

'I knew I shouldn't have left you alone this morning,' he said, his voice cool and reflective. 'What is it, Minerva?'

There was no tactful way of saying it. In a sharp, staccato voice she asked, 'Why did Stella kill herself?'

His silence forced her head around. He looked grim, yet resigned. 'I knew it had to come sooner or later,' he said tonelessly. 'I suppose I hoped that there would be time first to bind you more closely to me. Selfish, I'll admit, but I'm a selfish man.'

'I have to know,' she whispered, imploring him to understand.

'Why? Because you don't trust me?' The pale gaze was cruelly reflective. 'I can understand that, I suppose, although I damned well don't like it. Very well then. Stella killed herself for reasons that seemed good to her.

I don't know that she wanted you to know what they were.'

Eyes huge in her white face, Minerva shook her head. Disappointment clutched her stomach, sent icy chills through her taut body. 'I don't believe that,' she said raggedly.

'Then why didn't she make sure she told you?' he asked without expression, his gaze never leaving her face.

'*What was the matter with her*?' His controlled impassivity grated on nerves already rubbed raw by the shock of Stella's letter and the long, interminable day. 'Damn you, tell me!' she shouted, grabbing his shirt and shaking in a fury of rage and pain and despair. 'You must know! Why are you tormenting me like this?'

He didn't defend himself, merely looked at her with an expressionless face and icy, unblinking eyes. Minerva's hands stilled, but her hands clenched on his shirt, warm from the heat of his big body, as though it was a lifeline. Briefly, he closed his eyes.

'Yes, I know,' he admitted with harsh composure. 'It's quite simple, really. Humiliating, but simple. Stella couldn't bring herself to sleep with me. I assume that's what made her miserable; it certainly did me, especially when I realised that however patient I was we weren't ever going to get anywhere.'

Minerva's mouth dropped open. Her hands fell away. He looked big and angry, the slow fuse burned through at last, and rage beginning to gleam like fire beneath an opaque flow of lava.

'What?' she asked stupidly. Whatever she had dreaded, it wasn't this.

He showed strong white teeth in a snarl. 'You heard me. She would not go to bed with me.'

'But—why?'

'Who knows?' His hands clenched into fists. 'She wouldn't tell me, wouldn't talk about it at all, wouldn't talk to anyone else. I don't know whether she had any other reason than a sadistic pleasure in keeping me on a string. At first I thought she was a virgin, but she wasn't, was she?'

Slowly, Minerva shook her head. Stella hadn't been a virgin since she was sixteen. Her affairs had been light-hearted, but they had definitely been sexual.

'I'm glad you didn't lie.'

He had hauled in the reins on his temper and was once more speaking with an austere deliberation that tightened Minerva's skin. Her heart beat, light and fast, in her ears. Her mouth had dried; she couldn't speak, could only shake her head as though the action negated the truth of what he was saying.

Without looking at her as he said in cynical, measured tones, 'I was faced with tears and promises, stark terror and melting, little-girl provocation, and always the brick wall of her refusal. Shall I tell you how I know she wasn't a virgin?'

'It doesn't matter,' she croaked.

Ignoring her, he said through his teeth, 'A couple of months after we were married I overheard a conversation. A man I knew distantly was telling another what a hot little piece—yes, you can grimace but those were his words—my wife was. He'd slept with her on their first date, and she was everything he'd ever wanted. He envied me, although he thought I'd have my time cut out keeping her in my bed. Only he put it more crudely than that.'

'I'm sorry,' Minerva said beneath her breath, and reached up and touched his cheek, her sympathy obvious in her dark eyes and softly trembling mouth.

He flung her hand from him as though her touch poisoned him. 'I don't need your pity,' he said harshly. 'I don't need anything from you.'

Minerva couldn't prevent her involuntary recoil, but dismissing the pain, she asked tentatively, 'Did you tell her?'

'Oh, yes.' He showed his teeth again. 'To put it as crudely as he did, I told her that if she put it about so freely for others she could do the same for me.'

'And what happened?' Minerva asked almost inaudibly, too horrified at the images his words conjured up to realise that she had no right to ask such questions.

'She cried,' he said evenly, 'just as she cried every other time she refused me. And I discovered that, however much I wanted her, I couldn't rape a woman. Even if she was my wife. Especially when she was my wife.'

'Did you ask her to get help?'

Hooded eyes glittered molten beneath heavy lids; his smile was no more than a savage movement of his lips. 'She almost had hysterics at the thought. I suggested therapy, I tried to woo her into my bed, I begged, I pleaded, I was gentle and kind and unthreatening—she told me so herself—but nothing worked. She swore she loved me, she even said she wanted me, yet she wouldn't let me touch her, and, worse still, she wouldn't bloody well do anything about it! So I concluded she'd married me because she fancied my bank balance.'

'She wouldn't have married you if she hadn't wanted you.' Minerva's voice was completely positive. 'You weren't the first rich man to want to marry her, you know. You were special.'

'At first I thought so, too.' He leaned back, closing his eyes. 'Later, I realised that if she really did love me she would at least have been prepared to get help.'

Minerva bit her lip. Although part of her agreed, it wasn't going to help him if she said so.

'I thought she might have been raped,' he said levelly, 'but she swore that wasn't it. When it came to actually doing something about it, she refused every time. Eventually, I could only assume that she was getting some sort of sick pleasure out of the situation. It meant she had me dancing on tenterhooks, wooing her like a lapdog, paying court to her, yet not doing anything so sordid, so sweaty and primitive and *dirty* as actually taking her to bed.'

Minerva made a subdued sound of protest, but his bitter words had a ring of truth that kept her silent.

'In the end,' he said remotely, 'I got tired of pandering to her. I didn't hate her, I didn't love her, I was just totally sick of the wasteland our marriage had become. And then it was even worse. Because when she realised she couldn't torment me any longer, she started being provocative in a sly, childish way, as though it fed something in her to have me panting after her.'

Minerva fought back the nausea that burned in her throat. Jaggedly, she said, 'I can't believe this.'

But she did. She remembered the little-girl pose Stella had used, often at moments of great stress.

'And that,' he said with frigid distaste, 'sickened me even more. It happened whenever we had an argument—at least, whenever I argued. She never fought. She used to cry, then try to coax me into a good mood. I swear, sometimes I thought she was caught in a time warp. Yet there was this none too subtle invitation about her, as though the only way she knew to make things better was to invite a passion she had no intention of fulfilling.'

Minerva had to swallow before she could respond. 'That's sick.'

'It's the Stella I knew,' he said mercilessly. 'Are you telling me you don't recognise anything of her?'

Minerva's silence told him all he wanted to know. 'She hated quarrels,' she said lamely, as though it was some sort of excuse.

'I know.' Carefully he unclenched his hands, took a deep breath. 'That wasn't all that she hated.'

If Stella had wanted to torment him she should be happy wherever she was, because that was what he looked like, a soul in agony. The starkly etched angles and planes of his face were honed into a forbidding, blackly dangerous carving; there swirled about him such an air of threatening emotion that Minerva edged backwards.

But Stella hadn't wanted to torment him. Minerva would have staked her life on that. So there had to be another reason for her behaviour.

He said in a voice devoid of feeling, 'In the end, I told her I didn't want anything to do with her. That's why she killed herself. Because I told her I was sick of her. And because——'

'And because,' Minerva supplied jerkily when he stopped, 'you resumed your affair with Genevieve Chatswood.'

His head turned so that he could focus on her white, determined face. Through narrowed eyes he looked at her, the pale, opaque grey eaten up by a frightening anger. 'Who told you that?' he asked with slow, silky menace.

Minerva's stomach kicked into fear. Tightening her jaw, she held his gaze with a desperate composure. 'It doesn't matter.'

He shrugged, broad shoulders moving infinitesimally. 'Stella didn't know anything about Genevieve,' he said.

'How do you know?'

'Because when I had to go to Rotorua I didn't intend to sleep with Genevieve. Her parents offered me their house by the lake. Until I arrived I had no idea she was there.'

'Perhaps she told Stella.'

He shook his head. 'No. She's not stupid. I'd given her no encouragement—she would have gained nothing from telling Stella.'

Clearly he'd considered that possibility. Looking at the evidence logically, he was probably right. Genevieve Chatswood did not seem to be the sort of person who left anything to chance. She'd have made sure she had Nick well and truly seduced before she told Stella anything about it.

Minerva tried to speak objectively. 'I suppose I can understand why you—you——'

'Slept with her? That's generous of you,' he said softly. 'Tell me.'

Too late she understood what shaky ground she had trespassed on. 'It's none of my business,' she said, in full retreat.

'I rather think you've made the whole stinking shambles your business,' he said, smiling in a way that made every hair on her skin pull upright. 'Give me the benefit of your wisdom.'

Her voice died in her throat. Swallowing to ease the strain, she said shrilly, 'Because you were hungry, I suppose. Ten months is a long time for a man to remain celibate.'

'Don't forget the month before we married. Eleven months. Tell me, could you remain celibate for eleven months? Or are you like your sister, a provocative little tease with a penchant for tears and excuses?'

Minerva had grown so accustomed to Nick's ironclad restraint that she had forgotten the river of emotion beneath. It was a mistake.

She could not let him see how afraid she was. He had the instincts of a hunter, the need to drag down game that fled. Haughtily, she returned, 'We're not discussing me.'

'I've just changed the subject,' he said, looking at her with half-closed, speculative eyes. 'How many men have you slept with, Minerva? As many as your sister?'

Automatically, she shook her head, then, as guilt surged through her, hung it.

'So—how many?' He was playing with her, that beautiful, layered voice without inflexion, silver eyes as opaque and emotionless as the sea just before dawn.

'Mind your own business,' she said robustly, not taking her eyes from him because she felt safer that way, even though that chilling, fathomless gaze held her ensnared, trapped.

'It's just as much my business as the reason I went to bed with Genevieve is yours,' he said austerely. 'Have you any idea, I wonder, just what complete and utter rejection does? She gelded me, your beautiful sister. By the time she'd finished with me I no longer wanted her, or any woman. And there was Genevieve, and I knew she wanted me.'

He looked down at the glass in his hand and suddenly threw it with all his force against the fireplace. It shattered in a splintering explosion, shards of glittering crystal mingled with the amber drops of liquid.

Shocked, Minerva cried out, but he ignored her. 'Only I couldn't make it with Genevieve, either,' he said viciously. 'So technically I wasn't unfaithful to your sister. But that doesn't count, does it? Because the intention was certainly there.'

The broken glass forgotten, Minerva stared at him, her eyes dilating as she realised what he meant.

His smile was slow and cruel and explicit, as explicit as the look he gave her, running from the satiny tenderness of her mouth to the slight mounds of her breasts, thence on to the narrow indentation of her waist, the contours of hip and thigh beneath the material of her skirt, the slender calves his knowing fingers had massaged the night before, the small, elegantly poised feet.

Everywhere the polished sword of his gaze lingered pulse points sprang feverishly into life.

He said quietly, 'So you don't need to worry about me, Minerva. Didn't I prove that last night? I can touch you like this——' his finger traced the straight length of her eyebrow, lingered down the curve of her jaw and the pale column of her throat, leaving fire like a brand across her white skin '—and this, and nothing will happen.'

He caressed the smooth swell of her breast, finding the peak unerringly, scraping a thumb across it so that the aureole tightened into a small, excruciatingly sensitive bud.

His mouth widened in that parody of a smile. 'Yes, you like that,' he said, his voice deepening. 'But you don't have to worry. I can touch you,' and, with a movement so swiftly unexpected that she cried out, he brought her up against his hard body, 'without anything happening at all to upset your precious equilibrium.'

She flinched away, and he said gently against her lips, 'No, you don't have to pull back. This unruly part of me rises to a stimulus, but it's all lies, Minerva. When the time comes, it refuses to perform.'

When Minerva gasped, he kissed her, crushing her resistant mouth beneath his, ranging behind the fortress of her teeth to plunder the depths of her mouth with his tongue. Sensation, violent and fierce as a summer storm, shot through her like lightning. Something strange and unknown stirred in the pit of her stomach, quivered through her thighs and the secret parts of her body.

This was what she had feared, this yielding, this intensity. Since the episode with Paul Penn, Minerva had based her actions on common sense; it was more important than anything else in her life. It had saved her from uncounted stupidities.

Now, too late, she realised that it meant very little. She had always suspected her great capacity for passion, and been afraid to abandon herself to it. After that first abortive affair she had locked herself away, and no one had ever come close to luring her from behind the walls of her disillusion. But in trying to understand Nick she had concentrated so hard on him, searching every word, every fleeting expression for a meaning other than the obvious, an intonation she might have missed, going over and over his possible motives, that she had left herself wide open to him. Now she was helpless against his dark, powerful sorcery.

When he lifted his head he smiled into her bewildered eyes. 'You taste like life,' he said thickly, 'warm and sweet and female, but don't let that kiss alarm you, because although I can kiss you until we're both mindless with desire, can touch you with hands that ache with wanting, can take your breast in my mouth and forget everything for a few minutes but the honeyed taste of you, the truth is that I can't do anything else. I'm impotent, so you're quite safe from my crude, vulgar advances.'

She gasped and that terrible smile deepened. 'I won't slide between your legs and take you,' he said huskily, 'feel you close around me in the best sensation God ever invented, I won't lie on you and make you mine, I can't pump myself into you and forget for a few precious, reckless moments that life is ugly and hard and unfair. I'm useless as a lover, Minerva.'

One strong brown hand wrenched her shirt open, sending buttons popping in all directions, and he looked his fill at her slight curves. Colour heated her white skin, climbing all the way to her cheeks.

His smile was sardonic. 'It looks like the glow of climax.'

Minerva twisted frantically, desperate to put an end to this. With a deliberate show of strength he pulled her down on to the rug, holding her writhing, struggling body easily. Even hindered by the sleeves of her shirt she might have broken free, but her traitorous heart betrayed her, and when his mouth touched her breast she was reduced to abject, immediate surrender.

It was like nothing she had ever experienced, like the roaring of some great crowd gone mad with excitement and exaltation, like the slow, powerful pulse of the universe, pleasure beyond pleasure, sweeping her with it into a realm of experience as magnificent as life itself.

The fingers that threaded through the warm silk of his hair clenched, tried to pull his head away, and then yielded, holding him to her breast with an unconscious tenderness.

'You don't have to worry,' he said, his words tiny shocks on the acutely sensitive skin of her nipple. 'I can pull off your skirt like this and kiss you here, and here and here, but whatever I do, I can't take you. I can't fill you with me.'

His quick hands stripped her melting body of the last fragile barrier.

'But I can satisfy you,' he said, his voice guttural with strain. 'That's easy enough to do. You enjoyed what I did last night, didn't you? You have no idea what it did to me to hear your voice moaning and knowing that I was doing it to you.'

Minerva said uncertainly, 'Nick, I——'

'Don't!' His voice was anguished; he turned his face away, resting it between her breasts.

Minerva shuddered. A consuming savagery of need scored her with its talons. More than anything she wanted to ease his bitter torment; however, she knew enough about impotence to understand that it was highly unlikely she could help. He needed skilled therapy, not the amateur administrations of a woman whose only claim to effectiveness was that she loved him.

She couldn't let this go on.

'Take your clothes off,' she said gruffly.

He had been stroking from her waist to the spread of her hips, his touch gentle in spite of the calluses on his hand. At her command he lifted his head and looked at her. His eyes were cool and clear, almost dispassionate.

'It won't work,' he said casually.

Chin jutting, she snapped, 'I don't care about that. I haven't got any clothes on: I don't see why you should wear yours.'

Astonishingly, swift amusement glimmered in the moonlight depths of his eyes. 'Very well, then,' he said gravely. 'You want them off, you take them off.'

When it came to actually taking his shirt off she was seized with shyness. Carefully keeping her head down, she struggled with his uncooperative buttons until eventually she had them all free.

She had never realised that scent was so important. It hadn't been to her before. But as she pushed his shirt back she realised that the salty, clean scent she liked so much was the essence of his masculinity.

Her mouth dried. Beneath a light dusting of hair the lean, long muscles of hard physical exercise flexed under her wondering eyes. He was magnificent, the strength and power of maleness personified.

Slowly her hand crept out, touched him. He shuddered, sleek skin pulling taut under the sensitive tip of her finger. She looked up into his face, her own flushed and wondering.

'Yes,' he said hoarsely. 'Touch me, Minerva. I like it. I like your hands on me, I like your mouth on me, I'd like the little lash of your tongue on me...'

Long hair falling like an elegant waterfall across his chest, she pushed him against the back of the sofa so she could copy his actions, suckle at the small, male bud, taste the tangy flavour that was Nick. His heartbeat increased until all she heard was his breathing and the thunder of his heart, all she felt was his hand as it found the hidden inner part of her, moving with the skill and precision of experience to summon an undreamed of response.

Firelight gleamed golden on the delicate translucence of white skin, burnished his smooth hide into gleaming copper. The quiet room held its breath. When Minerva touched the hot skin of the man she loved, fire burned through her. She moved restlessly, her thigh rubbing against the steel sheet of his.

And then suddenly it became a matter of urgency, a need that refused to be denied. She kissed him, mouth sealed to mouth, and with gentle fingers discovered the masculine length of him. He groaned, but didn't move, although she could feel the rigid tension in every muscle. She hesitated, but a glance from beneath her lashes told her he wasn't going to help.

And that he wanted her every bit as fiercely as she wanted him. She pushed him down on to the thick cushions of the sofa, running her hands across him, her eyes glazed and slumbrous, her whole being caught up in the movement.

Somehow, without her knowing exactly how it happened, he slid inside her. He groaned something she couldn't hear, his eyes blazing. Firelight ran fingers of flame over a face that was hard and tense and drawn, the face of a man in agony.

His strength and potency burgeoned inside her, filling her, inciting her, until, compelled by age-old instincts, she moved above him, drawing him deeper and further in.

Slowly, hesitantly at first and then with increasing confidence, she set a pattern. Sensation built, licked through her in the leaping rhythm of the flames, soared higher and higher, until she cried out and crested, and crested again, and felt his body arch beneath her, the hands on her hips bite deeply into skin that would be bruised tomorrow. In the ecstasy of the moment she didn't even notice the cruel grip.

Shuddering, she collapsed on top of him, her head empty of anything but a languorous satiation, her body limp and boneless.

The fire died. Beneath her cheek Nick's thudding heart moderated, returned to normal. The swift chill of night began to creep across her skin, adding its strength to the icy spring that welled up through her.

She'd been conned before, she thought bleakly, but that had to be one of the neatest seduction routines she'd ever come across.

'You don't have to worry... I'm impotent.' And she'd fallen for it. Had it all been lies, Stella's frigidity as well?

Shivering, she began to free herself. Immediately his arms tightened.

'Thank you,' he said huskily.

Unable to look at him, she muttered, 'I'm cold,' and scrambled to her feet, scooping up her clothes as she fled behind the sofa.

She kept her head turned away, but from the sounds she could hear he was dressing, too, no doubt smirking about how easy it had been to get her into bed, she thought homicidally.

What did she do now? Run, her mind commanded.

But as she headed for the door, she was stopped by a hand on her upper arm. Nick turned her, gently but inexorably. Minerva kept her lashes lowered.

He'd pulled on his trousers, for which heaven be thanked, but hadn't got as far as his shirt. The breadth of his shoulders, the colours and textures of his torso, overwhelmed her. Her breath locked in her throat. Never before had she suffered this ruthless desire, this need to forget everything in the sensuous surcease only he could give her.

'Nick——' she began thinly.

He interrupted with a calmness she resented, 'Are you protected at all?'

'No.'

He bit back a curse. 'We have to talk,' he said.

'Not now, please.' She tried to hide the note of desperation in her voice, improvising freely as she added, 'I—I'm exhausted.'

She felt the track of his gaze across her face. 'All right,' he said, not trying to hide his reluctance. 'Tomorrow morning.' It was a promise, not a suggestion.

Without speaking, she nodded, and went out into the darkness and up to her room.

She waited until the clock in the hall chimed three, and then, carrying her pack, slid through the silent, unlit homestead and out to the garage. No dogs barked, not then and not as she drove away down the gravel road towards Auckland.

When she arrived home dawn had broken and her stepmother was speaking into the telephone. 'Oh,' she said, looking puzzled as she put her hand over the mouthpiece. 'It's Nick. He wants to talk to you, darling.'

Minerva said wearily, 'I don't want to talk to him.'

Ruth's puzzlement intensified to bewilderment. 'Why, darling?'

'I just don't.'

Ruth's eyes searched her face. Minerva knew what she could see: pallor, dark circles, signs of strain she couldn't hide.

'All right,' her stepmother said quickly, 'I'll tell him you got here safely.'

Minerva steadied her pack on the floor and listened to Ruth speak to Nick in her warm, affectionate voice. 'Yes, she's here. No, Brian is already at work—disgusting, isn't it? All right...'

Leaving her pack propped against the wall, Minerva went slowly upstairs to her room. When Ruth knocked she was sitting on the window seat with Stella's letter in her hand. She handed it over, saying tonelessly, 'It arrived yesterday.'

As soon as she saw Stella's handwriting Ruth turned white and groped her way into a chair. She looked at Minerva as though she had suddenly grown a green beard. 'What does it say?' she whispered.

'You'd better read it.'

She breathed calmly, deeply while Ruth read it. When her sweet, unfailingly kind stepmother swore, the ugly curse sounding even uglier in her soft voice, Minerva jerked with shock.

'Ruth!'

'Oh, God, I wish I'd killed him,' she said in a frozen voice, looking past Minerva at something too horrible to contemplate.

'What did he do?' Minerva asked tightly. When Ruth didn't answer, she demanded, 'Ruth, what did Nick do?'

'Nick?' Now Ruth looked at her, the torment and fury in her eyes overlaid by blank astonishment. 'What are you talking about? Nick didn't do anything. It was her father.'

And suddenly everything, Stella's promiscuity, her fragility, her inability to sleep with Nick, even the childishness he found so repelling, blended into a horrible comprehension in Minerva's appalled mind.

'Her father?' she whispered, sickened.

The ready tears sprang to her stepmother's eyes. 'Yes,' she said in a hard little voice. 'That's why I divorced him. It had been going on for a year before I found out.'

'Oh, God!'

'Yes, my poor little Stella. She was only a baby, and he—and he——' Ruth began to weep in earnest.

'Her—her own—father?' Minerva said disconnectedly, speaking only because she had to say something; silence was too dreadful to be endured.

Ruth's hands jerked at her pretty handkerchief. 'Yes. Her own father.'

Minerva went across and knelt beside her, taking the restless hands in hers, her eyes suddenly weighted and hot. 'Oh, Ruth. What a dreadful thing for you. And for Stella. Poor, poor Stella.'

Ruth began to weep again. Minerva hugged her, held her tight, and stared sightlessly across the expensively furnished room.

'She said she was all right,' her stepmother said eventually, her voice choked with grief. 'She seemed fine, and all the time she was so terribly, terribly wrong. My poor baby...'

They mourned for long moments, two women united by a wrenching, unresolved grief, until Minerva said, choosing her words carefully, 'You'll have to tell Nick. He deserves to know.'

She felt Ruth's involuntary withdrawal even before she said, 'Oh, I couldn't. I couldn't. He'd blame me.'

'Why should he blame you?'

She pressed her handkerchief to her eyes. 'I should have noticed. If I'd been a better mother——'

'Don't give me that rubbish!' Looking deep into her stepmother's eyes, Minerva shook her slightly. 'You were all that any child needed. You're not responsible for what a pervert did. Did you stay on in the marriage after you knew?'

Ruth's face mirrored her shocked revulsion. 'No. Oh, no. I went to the police. He spent years in prison—he died there. But I'd divorced him long before that.'

'Then why should anyone blame you?'

Her stepmother shook her head. 'If I'd seen that she had some sort of counselling,' she began. 'But when she was young there wasn't anything like that, and anyway, the doctor I consulted told me she'd get over it. Then later, when we heard more about incest and its devastating effects, I suggested she see someone, a doctor, somebody, but she laughed at me. She said she was all right, she didn't need to see a shrink.'

Minerva thrust down her own reservations. It was no use blaming Ruth; she had done what she could for her daughter.

Ruthlessly sacrificing Stella's memory, she said briskly, 'She was twenty-six, old enough to take control of her own life. Even if she couldn't bear to tell Nick, she could have worked through it with professional help before marrying him. I know I sound hard, but she—because she couldn't bring herself to do that, she made Nick a victim of her father, too. You owe it to him to tell him.'

Ruth bit her lip, but she nodded. 'Yes,' she said humbly. 'You're right, of course.'

Minerva looked significantly towards the telephone.

'Oh, but——' A picture of indecision, Ruth hesitated, before asking pathetically. 'Can I get myself a cup of tea first?'

'I'll get it for you.' Minerva gave her a quick hug. 'It wasn't your fault,' she said sternly. 'If it was anyone's fault it was the man who did that to her. She wouldn't have wanted you to blame yourself, you know that!'

'I failed her.'

Minerva released her. 'You did not,' she said as they headed off towards the kitchen.

By the time Ruth had drunk her tea it was obvious she wasn't going to be able to tell Nick anything. One of her migraines had come on, and all Minerva could do was take her up to her room, tuck her in with the curtains drawn, and sit holding her hand until eventually she sank into a deep sleep. When she woke the headache would be gone, and, although she would be frail and shaky, she would be able to cope.

But probably not with telling Nick, Minerva thought, walking out on to the terrace at the back of the house. Everywhere the gentle radiance of spring was in full splendour, from the mist of violet-blue buds on the huge jacaranda beside the pool to the homely charm of pink and white and yellow and blue daisies.

She was unable to take her usual comfort from the ordered disorder of Ruth's garden, so cunningly and carefully achieved. So much had happened, so many shocks, that her thoughts and emotions whirled chaotically.

But it didn't really matter; Nick's manner when he'd told her about his marriage made it more than obvious that he was not yet over the wife he had both loved and hated. And until that happened he had nothing to offer, except a sexuality that was somehow mechanical.

Physically he was all that a woman could want from a man, at once tender and fierce, controlled and wildly passionate, but now Minerva wondered whether she had been used, if any woman would have done.

Stella. It all came back to Stella. Nick was going to have to deal with his brief, heartbreaking marriage before he could even think of a relationship with any other woman. Locked in the past, he was held unwilling prisoner by his memories.

A cold melancholy crept over Minerva. Shivering, she stood with her arms across her chest, eyes fixed unseeingly on the garden, until slowly, inevitably, she became aware that she was not alone.

CHAPTER SIX

IT WAS no shock to see Nick's tall figure motionless inside the wide French windows.

Stonily, she asked, 'How did you get here?'

'I flew down.' Like hers, his voice revealed nothing but polite neutrality. He came out on to the terrace. 'Why all the drama? You didn't really have to run away.'

Minerva wasn't prepared to answer that. With a quick glance up at the firmly closed curtains of Ruth's room, she summoned her courage and said flatly, 'I know why Stella wouldn't sleep with you.'

'Why?'

Her mouth trembled. Gazing blindly at the sensuous curves and colours of the roses, she breathed in their warm, evocative scent, and in an emotionless voice told him.

Silence stretched unbearably between them, until he ground out a curse and smashed his fist on the railing with such force that she winced. He didn't seem to realise what he had done; in a dreadful monotone he called the man who had abused Stella every foul name he knew.

Then he stopped. The distant hum of the traffic receded into silence. Wishing that she could help him with his grief, fighting her own, Minerva realised that Stella, her wasted life and lonely, heartbreaking death, would be a barrier between them forever. Even if the unlikely happened and Nick learned to love her, Minerva, there was no way she could build any degree of happiness on the foundations of her sister's memory.

She said wearily, 'I'm sorry.'

'How did you find out?'

In a monotone she told him of the letter and Ruth's reaction to it.

'I see,' he said when she had finished. 'How's Ruth?'
'Shattered.'

He said in an anguished voice, 'Why didn't Stella tell me? For God's sake, she can't have thought I'd blame her?'

'I don't know.' She hesitated, then ploughed on. 'I think I can understand why she behaved the way she did, though. Stella always wanted everything to be picture-perfect. She hated dirt, or mess of any sort. I can see why, now. The men she slept with weren't important, so it didn't mean anything to her. But you—you were everything to her. She loved you. And she...'

The words trailed into silence. She swallowed the painful lump in her throat, composed her voice again. '...and she loved her father.'

'Are you suggesting that she somehow got me confused with what her——? No! I don't believe it!' Repugnance roughened his voice.

'No, not that. Just that love and pain, love and degradation were so mixed up her mind that she couldn't separate them.'

'You must be wrong,' he snarled.

But her words had struck home. She couldn't think of anything she could say that might ease the self-disgust she saw in his expression.

Eventually he said heavily, 'I'm sorry, you're probably right. It fits. It seems so obvious now, but at the time it never occurred to me. Not even when I was nearly mad with wondering what was wrong. When I told her I was no longer interested, it must have been the ultimate betrayal. And she could think of nothing to do but swallow those bloody pills.'

Minerva's heart ached with compassion. Quickly, because it was too painful to think about, she said, 'There was something else, too, wasn't there? Jillian told me she found her sobbing in the car a few days before she killed herself. She'd just been to see the doctor.'

'He'd told her she couldn't have children,' Nick said in a dead voice.

'It would have stopped a hell of a lot of gossip if you'd told them at the inquest,' she said bitterly. 'Ruth would have been able to cope with that. She might even have understood it, instead of blaming herself.'

'It was Stella's business, not anything for the public to gossip over.' He paused, then said, 'Ruth knew.'

Understanding at last, Minerva drew in a sharp breath. All this time she had thought Ruth was in agony because she didn't know why her daughter had committed suicide. And all the time her stepmother had blamed herself for not realising that Stella needed help.

And, perhaps, for not preventing the abuse all those years ago.

Minerva snatched a swift glance at Nick. His face was carved in stone, suddenly much older, lines engraved deeply at the corners of his mouth and his eyes. Very quietly, she said, 'Stella loved you, Nick. Don't ever believe that she didn't.'

'Unfortunately she didn't love me enough to get the help she must have known was the only way to salvage our marriage, did she?'

The question was unanswerable. Minerva's composure was crumbling, tearing itself to shreds, but she had to stay calm, because this was the only way to help him.

'We weren't at all alike, Stella and I, but we loved each other. Yet it was always me who looked after her. She was—I can't think of any word to describe her except fragile, and that isn't really right. I think she felt powerless. You're not to blame, neither is Ruth, neither is Stella. Oh, I'd like to kill her father!'

'You wouldn't have a chance,' he said between gritted teeth.

Minerva's blood ran cold. For a mercifully brief moment she saw a man capable of murder. If Stella's father had still been alive Nick would have killed him as quickly and relentlessly as one killed a mad dog.

'In the meantime,' he said in an inflexible voice, 'we have another, more immediate problem. What are you going to do if last night left you pregnant?'

She had vaguely considered the possibility as she drove away from Spanish Castle, but since then it hadn't even entered her head. Now she said stiffly, 'I don't know.'

His hands on her shoulders were a shocking intrusion. She went rigid, holding herself erect, trying to show him with her level gaze that she was not intimidated. He looked like a statue beaten from pure metal, the angular features compelling and forceful. The sun burnished his hair into gold, but beneath his straight brows his eyes were the transparency of crystals, hard, without the slightest warmth.

'If there's a child,' he said coolly, 'I want it. Don't abort it.'

The colour seeped from her skin. 'What would you do with a child?'

'I'm not likely to marry again,' he replied indifferently, 'unless it's to have children. If you have one I can save myself from that. And perhaps another woman from more pain.'

He couldn't have hurt her more if he had tried. To have the death knell of her inchoate hopes sounded so clearly was a sharp agony. Fighting to keep her face blank, she drew a shallow, painful breath. 'If I'm pregnant,' she promised, 'I'll let you know.'

His teeth showed a moment in a brief, unamused smile. 'You'd better,' he said.

His hands dropped. Turning away, he walked out of her life.

She left for the Virgin Islands a week later than she intended to. When Ruth at last told her husband why Stella had killed herself, she collapsed and spent a week in bed, a week during which it seemed she might finally succumb to the nervous breakdown that had been threatening for so long.

However, she didn't. She even managed to convince herself that she was all right, although she convinced no one else. It took the combined efforts of Minerva and her father to get her to attend a group recommended by her doctor, and even then Minerva wondered whether she should stay and see her through this traumatic time.

It was her father who convinced her to pick up her own life. One night after Ruth had gone to bed, he said, 'When are you going?'

'I thought perhaps I should stay for a while.'

'No. You've spent enough of your life helping people through pain,' he said unexpectedly. 'I remember how good you were when your mother died. Then you welcomed Ruth and Stella, and eased Ruth through learning how to be a stepmother and Stella through the torments of her adolescent years. Ruth is a leaner; she needs a lot of support. Stella was the same. Not like you: you're an independent, always have been, with a heart too soft for your own good. But you've your own life to live.'

She smiled bleakly. Although summer was still flirting on the edges of the year, the night was warm. They were sitting in the conservatory with the doors open so that the scents of the garden drifted in.

'If you think that Ruth doesn't need me ...'

Brian Robertson smiled and patted her hand. 'Oh, she needs you. But she has me. You go and learn to feel young again.'

She looked at him in astonishment. 'How do you know I feel so old I think I may never laugh again?'

'I know you,' he said quietly. 'How long is your contract?'

'Only for a year.'

'Come back then.'

She nodded. 'All right, I will.'

*   *   *

A year later, at the end of November, she did. Everyone—Ruth, the schoolfriends she still kept in touch with, her father—had mentioned the warm, wet spring in their letters, so she wasn't surprised at the verdant green of Northland's long spine. It was green, greener than any other green, glowing beneath the warm sun. As the great aircraft measured the length of the narrow peninsula Minerva thought she saw the Spanish Castle.

It was ridiculous, of course; there were plenty of rocky peaks in Northland. She had no idea how Nick was. The only news she had of him was when Ruth mentioned him in her letters, which wasn't often, and only in passing.

Once she had known she wasn't pregnant she had written him a formal, stilted letter, then waited with embarrassing and humiliating eagerness for his answer. It had been cool and impersonal: he wished her well. He was hers sincerely, Nick.

It had hurt almost as much as his first rejection.

'I always forget how absolutely beautiful it is,' said the woman next to her. 'However jet-lagged I am, I can still look down and feel a surge of patriotic fervour.' She smiled in self-derision, but her eyes lingered compulsively on the complex intermingling of land and sea below.

'I know what you mean.' They had exchanged some casual conversation on the eleven and a half hour flight from Los Angeles, but both of them had spent most of the time asleep.

'Is anyone meeting you?' the older woman asked.

'Oh, my stepmother and father will be there. Ruth is convinced that anyone arriving home from overseas will be mortally wounded if they're not met by a welcoming party, even if it means the welcoming party has to get up at some ungodly hour to be at the airport by seven in the morning.'

After a couple of months Ruth's letters had become so cheerful that Minerva hadn't needed her father's reassurances. Even when Kane was chosen to spend a year in America on a Rotary scholarship, Ruth's spirits had continued buoyant.

Minerva's lips curved. Apparently her half-brother had grown from a respectable five feet ten to a towering six feet two in the year she had been away. Ruth's letters had been full of alarmed references to girls who, it appeared, chased him unmercifully.

I'll bet he doesn't run very fast, his sister thought with wry amusement.

Twenty minutes later the plane was at Mangere Airport and for the first time in a year Minerva was engulfed by family and friends. Laughing, her eyes sparkling with pleasure and a few stray tears, she kissed everyone impartially, and was swept off home.

There was an air of unreality about the next week. The weather stayed at its mellow best, calm and warm and languid, and people surged through the house in waves of varying strength to welcome her home.

Minerva caught up on her sleep, went to the annual dinner of her class at boarding-school, parties with friends of her own and her parents', did a lot of laughing and reminiscing, and listened to gossip about people she knew and people she didn't.

But none about Nick. No one mentioned him at all. As the days passed without his name turning up in the conversation she began to wonder whether it was a conspiracy.

At last she asked casually, 'How's Nick? Or do you not see him at all now?'

'Nick? Oh, he's fine.' Ruth beamed. 'Darling, how long do you intend to stay this time? And don't you think it's time you settled down here with a nice man and gave us some grandchildren?' She smiled to show she was only teasing.

'I thought I might have a holiday,' Minerva said. She closed her eyes and let the dazzle from the swimming-pool dance across the ends of her lashes. Adroitly avoiding the subject of husband and family, she murmured, 'Until the summer is over, anyway. Then I might see about the Antarctic. I've never been there, and I rather fancy staying over the winter.'

It worked. After Ruth had asserted that anyone who wanted to spend one of the long, dark Antarctic winters on the ice-bound continent had to be mad, if not actually certifiable, the conversation drifted to other subjects.

But later, when her stepmother had bustled away to organise lunch, Minerva lay supine in the hammock suspended between two big branches of the jacaranda tree and wondered why she had given up on the idea of marriage. She still loved Nick, but any thought of marriage had been eclipsed by a hard-won, pragmatic acceptance that too much stood between them for any hope of a future together.

Perhaps she was meant to be single, she thought sleepily. After all, it had lots of advantages. Her life was satisfying and she was in complete control of it. She could do what she wanted, where she wanted, for as long as she wanted, and be paid extremely well for it.

When she was tired of wandering she could settle down and run her own restaurant and earn herself a brilliant reputation for excellent food served with flair and imagination. Make a decent income, too. Compared with that prospect, servitude to some man didn't hold many attractions.

Tears sparkled on the end of her lashes.

Several nights later she went with her parents to a very upmarket reception which celebrated the launching of a line of kiwi-fruit products. Her father was an exporter, and he'd contracted to handle the overseas marketing for the line. Minerva, who had spent the preceding two days with a friend on Waiheke, one of Auckland's many gulf islands, didn't arrive home until after Ruth and Brian had left. Surfeited with sun and sea and swimming, she was sorely tempted to make a snack and have an early night, but the evening was important to her father, so she showered, donned a pretty dress the same blue as her eyes, and caught a taxi to the luxury hotel where the reception was being held.

Somewhat to her surprise Minerva enjoyed herself. She renewed acquaintance with a variety of people, a few of whom she was pleased to see, giggled inconspicuously with Ruth over some of the more extreme fashions, and checked out the food with her professional eye and tastebuds.

Mentally tucking ideas away for future reference, she went off to repair her lipstick, and was emerging from behind a row of potted palms when her astonished eyes fell on the tall man with hair the colour of manuka honey who was standing a few feet away talking to a woman. The bottom of Minerva's stomach dropped away.

Nick. And Genevieve Chatswood. But after that first dismayed glance Minerva ignored his companion to stare hungrily at Nick.

Something sharp and consuming clutched the base of her spine. He looked the same, she thought, trying to clear her head of the fog that had infiltrated her thought processes. Those broad shoulders and long muscles set him apart as nothing else could. They were developed by hard, unremitting work, whereas the men around him acquired theirs in gyms.

He was three-quarters turned away, so all she could see was the chiselled line of his cheek and jaw, the proud carriage of his burnished head. And the relaxed, easy stance, the unaffected, disciplined authority that cast such a potent spell.

She froze as he turned and looked straight at her. It was darker behind the screen of palms, and the fronds were dense enough to prevent him from seeing her, but it seemed for one tense moment that his icy gaze cut right through the foliage to hold her transfixed like a hare in a searchlight. Then Genevieve Chatswood said something to him, and he looked away, and smiled at her.

A surge of pure, unadulterated animal need, a primitive and elemental response to his untrammelled masculinity, swept over Minerva, drowning every rational thought.

Dear heaven, she thought in furious despair, why not just shout 'Me Jane, you Tarzan', and get it over with?

When someone murmured, 'Excuse me?' from behind, she was recalled with abrupt brutality to her surroundings.

'Oh. Sorry,' she said, and set off towards the spot where she had left her father and Ruth.

She should have been inconspicuous. After all, there were about five hundred people there, almost all of them dressed in more impressive clothes, many of them infinitely better looking than she was. But the malignant spirit of coincidence held strong. Threading her way through the crowd at least ten feet away from Nick, her face determinedly averted, she suddenly felt the full force of his personality, and knew that he had seen her. Leashing her almost uncontrollable urge to glance his way, she walked on.

Scarcely two steps later, he said from behind, 'Minerva.'

She felt cut out like an animal from the herd, isolated, every instinct demanding that she run. Her throat closed; lifting her head proudly, she met his glance head on.

Cool grey eyes, as clear and depthless as glass, held hers. He wasn't smiling. He wasn't, she thought confusedly, anything. There was no flicker of emotion in his expression. It was impossible to believe that this man had ever lain beneath her while she took her pleasure of his body, impossible to remember the shocking rapture.

'Nick,' she said calmly. Her voice might have wobbled if she hadn't been concentrating so hard on keeping it steady. 'How are you?'

If he was amused by the banality of her response he didn't show it. 'I'm fine. And you?'

He filled her gaze, the black and white of his evening clothes suiting his tall, lean good looks, setting off the tanned face and rich amber hair. No matter how old she became, however resigned to her loss, she would always be threatened by that powerful male magnetism. Men like Nick weren't known as heartbreakers for nothing.

But she wasn't going to let him see that. Pasting a smile to lips that stretched unbearably, she replied, 'Oh, I'm very well. I didn't know you had interests in kiwi-fruit.'

'I bought an orchard in the euphoria of the eighties,' he said drily. 'When the bottom dropped out of the market I organised some of the venture capital to get this going.'

She nodded, trying to look as though his words meant something. Every scrap of small talk had deserted her.

A voice from beside Nick said briskly, 'Well, if it isn't—ah, Miranda, isn't it?' Genevieve Chatswood gave Minerva the kind of look that didn't have to be decoded. Keep off, it said loud and clear.

The other woman's arrival gingered Minerva's brain cells into activity. Stupidly and unregenerately glad that she had worn a dress that matched the colour of her eyes, she returned Genevieve's narrow smile. 'Minerva, actually. Hello,' she said. 'How are you? And how are the orchids?'

Genevieve looked a little taken aback, but answered readily enough. Minerva stood exchanging platitudes for a few minutes, before saying, 'I must go. I can see Ruth peering around wondering where I am. She won't wear her spectacles when she's out so she isn't able to see me, but it won't stop her from trying.'

'We'll go with you. I haven't seen Ruth or Brian tonight,' Nick said smoothly, apparently not noticing her swiftly hidden dismay.

Ruth greeted them all with her usual affectionate fuss, and for several minutes they stood talking. Genevieve obviously knew both Ruth and her husband reasonably well. Odd, Minerva thought ironically, that she should be the one who felt the outsider.

'And what are you doing home again, Minerva?' Genevieve asked in a lull in the conversation, stressing the penultimate word in a manner that Minerva found irritating.

'I'm back for the holidays,' she replied.

Smiling teasingly, her father said, 'Minerva's a nomad; she'll be off again soon. No place can hold her for long.'

Minerva grinned back at him. 'Actually, it's all a plot by my father to expand New Zealand's exports. I use a lot of New Zealand products when I cook.'

Ruth said proudly, 'Minerva has worked for some fascinating people.'

'How intriguing. Do you have much to do with your employers?' Genevieve asked, her sweet tone almost masking the sting. 'You must have some tales to tell.'

Minerva shrugged. 'I only work for people who are serious about good food, so I usually do see quite a lot of them when we discuss menus, and so on. But you're right,' smiling innocently at the woman opposite, 'I don't socialise with them. Difficult as it is for a New Zealander, I know my place.'

'Oh, I didn't mean——' Genevieve was clearly not accustomed to having her thrusts parried with such ruthless efficiency. She gave a small laugh and glanced up at Nick as though seeking help.

Minerva looked enquiringly at her. Genevieve said a little curtly, 'I didn't mean to offend you.'

'You didn't,' Minerva said, smiling. 'I'm not in the habit of taking offence, and I've been insulted by experts.'

Ruth rushed in to cover the awkwardness with small talk. That, Minerva thought with a satisfaction not untinged by malice, will warn madam butter-wouldn't-melt-in-her-mouth not to have a go at me again.

An irresistible compulsion forced her glance away from her stepmother to Nick. He was standing with his head inclined, listening with grave courtesy to Ruth. As though her glance was tangible, he looked at Minerva through half-closed lids. His mouth hardened.

She stared mulishly back. If he didn't want his little toy roughed up he should teach her some manners.

Deep in his eyes something flickered, a darkness that was hotter than fire, a hidden emotion that sent forbidden shock waves through the charged moment.

Although panic iced through her veins she refused to drop her gaze. There is no future for us, she thought sturdily. None at all. He loved Stella. Probably still does. If he marries Genevieve it will be because he wants children.

Minerva wanted children too, but unfortunately the children she wanted were Nick Peveril's.

That maddeningly turned-up corner to his mouth twisted. He looked away, and it was as though a leash had snapped.

Damn, she thought shakily. *Why me?* And why, of all people, does it have to be him?

Fortunately he and Genevieve left soon afterwards. They had promised to call in and see friends who were having a party.

Ruth smiled benignly after them. 'It would be so nice if they married,' she said.

To her horror Minerva found that her fingers were curling into claws. Carefully, as Ruth's voice prattled on about Genevieve's manifold virtues, she straightened her hands out and stared fixedly at the little red crescents her short, unpainted, practical nails had made in her palm.

'Do you think she's the right woman for him?' Minerva didn't know where the question came from. It certainly hadn't been in her mind when she opened her mouth. Perhaps it was simply that the thought of Nick marrying anyone still had the power to stab right through her stoical renunciation and hit some vital spot in her heart.

'As right as anyone, I suppose.' Ruth hesitated before saying earnestly, 'I certainly won't resent any woman Nick marries. There was a time, darling, when I even resented you, because you were alive and Stella was dead. Wicked and so irrational of me, wasn't it? But I'm over that now. My support group was such a help. I've finally accepted that Stella is dead, and that perhaps we did all fail her, but we did the best we could at the time. Life goes on, and Nick's sensible enough to realise it. Genevieve will do him very well. He needs a nice, practical girl who won't get angry because he loves Spanish Castle. Stella used to feel a little abandoned because he spent so much time out working on the station.'

Minerva knew she should leave the subject, but it was like a sore tooth, dragging her attention away from everything else.

'They do seem well suited,' she said, hoping Ruth would deny it.

'They do, don't they? It helps that they enjoy a similar lifestyle.'

Obviously Nick had well and truly got over his impotence. Minerva stared blindly around the room. Misery warred with outrage; ruthlessly, she drove them both out by telling herself that she only wanted Nick to be happy. Genevieve deserved him after waiting all this time. He deserved her, too.

Ruth laughed lightly. 'Of course, at one time I hoped—oh, look, there's Judy! I haven't seen her for years! What do you think she's wearing on her head? It looks like a cabbage, but I don't think it can be, do you?'

The reception wound down at midnight, but Minerva was hailed by a group of friends going on to a nightclub, and, because her heart was sore and she wanted to forget that Nick and Genevieve were somewhere together, she allowed herself to be waylaid.

Almost immediately she realised she was not going to enjoy herself. The music was too loud, the floor too crowded; one male member of the party was amorously drunk, and she was not in the mood for avoiding groping octopus hands and heavy innuendoes. Pleading exhaustion, she left in a taxi for home.

It wasn't until she was preparing for bed that she remembered Ruth's interrupted remark.

What had her stepmother hoped? Something that had embarrassed her a little; Minerva recognised the note in her voice.

She patted make-up remover over her face, not even seeing her reflection in the mirror as she recalled the wild impact of the moment she had seen Nick through the palm fronds. It was all very well to convince herself half a world away that she had accepted the situation, but reality was another thing.

At that first, unexpected glimpse her mouth had dried and her brain emptied and she'd remembered with Technicolor vividness making love with him. Even now, her body clenched as the same sweet fire flowed through her. But that wasn't all. She felt a quickening, as though she had been dead, and woken again. It hurt; she preferred the serenity of relinquishment.

She screwed on the top of the tube and set it down, picked up a cotton-wool ball and with swift, practised strokes began wiping off the remnants of her make-up. In the merciless eye of her mind she saw Nick as he had been the last night at Spanish Castle, magnificent in the pride of his masculinity, a formidable, dominant challenge to any woman.

Her body sprang to life, making her scandalously aware of the way her thoughts were tending. Biting her lip, she turned away from the mirror. She couldn't go to bed like this; she'd never sleep.

It took only a few moments to wrap one of the big bath towels around her bra and pants and slip down the stairs. She'd swim this attack off, she thought, trying to be blasé, striving to forget that somewhere not too far away Nick was probably making love to Genevieve Chatswood with flair and passion and skill. And cold-blooded mastery, because, although he might intend to marry the woman, he'd shown no signs of being in love with her.

Accustomed as Minerva was to warm Caribbean seas, the cooler water in the pool made her draw in a shocked breath. Gritting her teeth, she plunged completely in, swimming with steady, relentless strokes, length after length.

When at last she was exhausted, the light in her parents' room had long gone out, leaving only the moon, cool and pale and passive, to light her. Shivering, she climbed out and bent over to towel her hair with sharp, vicious strokes. It would take her at least half an hour to reduce it to order with a drier. One day, she decided, she'd cut it.

The memory of Genevieve's distinguished shoulder-length locks, superbly set, flickered across her mind to be instantly dismissed.

After a last, vigorous rub she stood up, flicking the heavy mass over her shoulders with a quick movement of her head then directed her gaze straight into Nick's face. For a frozen instant she stayed motionless, her wide eyes scanning his carved features with a terror that held nothing of logic. Then instinct kicked in and she leapt back.

Her heel slipped over the coping of the pool; flailing wildly, she teetered, and was almost over when he grabbed her, his hands warm and firm around her arms, and pulled her back.

'Easy, easy,' he said, his deep voice soft and slow, for all the world as though he were gentling a horse.

Minerva's heart was jumping out of control in her breast; she pressed her clenched fist over it, holding it in, and demanded in a voice that shook, 'Why on earth didn't you tell me you were there?'

'I'm sorry.' He didn't sound sorry, and he didn't release her, either. He had taken off the dinner-jacket and his cufflinks, rolled his sleeves halfway up his forearms. He looked big and forbidding and watchful, his hard-edged countenance delineated lovingly by the gentle moonlight, the icy blaze of his eyes impossible to meet as he scanned her face. 'I've just arrived.'

Which reminded her she had only a bra and pants on, both almost certainly transparent. Heat flooded her skin. With jerky swiftness she pulled the damp towel around her body, folding the overlap into the top across her breasts, thankful that she had brought one of the huge swimming sheets; it came almost to her knees.

'Are you all right?' he asked, letting her go.

'Yes.' She stepped away. 'What are you doing here?' she demanded, shivering.

'I'm spending the night here,' he said sardonically. 'Didn't Ruth tell you?'

'No. No, she hasn't had time, I suppose. I've been away the last couple of days.' In spite of an effort at detachment there was a grim note in her voice that promised enquiries later.

His teeth flashed white. 'I often stay here when I'm down for the night. How were the Virgin Islands?'

'They were fine. Very warm. Tropical.' She ended vaguely, 'Lots of coconut palms.'

'You must be noticing the difference in the temperature,' he said gravely.

He was laughing at her. As well he might; she was behaving like a gormless twit.

Racked by another sudden shiver, she turned towards the house.

'Yes, it's much cooler, but I like it,' she said numbly. 'Is Genevieve with you?'

The overwhelming physical response he always summoned was embarrassing, but she could cope with the thudding heart and the parched mouth and the clutch of desire in her stomach, the way her skin tightened and became abnormally sensitive. What was really upsetting was the effect he had on her thought patterns. His presence scrambled them entirely.

'No. She's staying with her parents.'

So perhaps they hadn't made love. Although if Jillian had been right with her nasty little bit of gossip of a year ago, Genevieve's parents were the broadminded sort. That being so, why wasn't he with them?

'I prefer to stay,' he continued calmly as though reading her mind, 'with my own family.'

Minerva was beginning to dislike that word. She hated being considered as merely one of his extended family. It was no consolation to know that Genevieve probably hated it just as much as she did.

'How long will you be home this time?' He asked it quite casually, his tone that of a person who was indulging in a little polite conversation.

She had to think hard to remember what she planned to do. 'Probably until the end of February,' she said after a noticeable pause. 'In New Zealand, that is. After Christmas I'm going to stay a while with friends in Central Otago. I've almost decided to see whether I can get a job cooking for one of the research stations in Antarctica.'

The straight brows lifted. 'Antarctica?'

Something in his tone brought her chin up. 'I'm a cook, remember,' she said curtly. 'I imagine one thing scientists in Antarctica really need is good food. Especially over the winter.'

'Yes. Would they take you on?'

'Why not?'

He smiled sardonically. 'I'm trying to put this tactfully. Aren't they rather careful about the personnel they let winter over? Beautiful woman must be a hazard to everyone's peace of mind, especially during the long dark months of winter when any diversion must be more than welcome.'

Her lip curled. She said brusquely, 'I'm not beautiful, and I have a rooted aversion to being considered a diversion, if that's what you were implying.'

Eyes unfathomable beneath the thick fringe of his lashes, he looked down at her proud profile. 'No,' he said thoughtfully, 'I wasn't.'

'I don't enjoy cheap compliments.'

'Do you get them often?' A note of amusement in his voice set her teeth gritting together. 'What's the difference between a cheap compliment and an expensive one? No, don't answer that. Instead, tell me why you're so convinced you're not attractive.'

'Stella was beautiful,' she returned remotely. 'And cheap compliments merely make me think that some men will try anything to get a woman into bed.'

They had reached the house. Short of running off she couldn't avoid him, and after the betraying stupidity of that last remark she wasn't going to run.

Come to think of it, she wouldn't be able to get away even if she did run; his long legs would cover the ground a lot faster than hers, and he knew the place well.

'Yes, Stella was beautiful,' he said, nothing but a reminiscent calmness in his voice. 'But there are different sorts of beauty. Many men would find your quiet strength equally appealing. And I'm sure I don't need to tell you that you have magnificent eyes and a mouth that is so controlled a man might see it as a challenge.'

Something mischievous and daring inside Minerva squirmed to struggle free. She squelched it. 'You're very flattering,' she said in her most withdrawn voice.

He laughed beneath his breath. 'And you don't believe a word of it. Some man certainly did a number on you, didn't he? Who was he?'

She repressed the memory of Paul's facile, lying compliments, and her own wondering, thrilled stupidity in believing them, because she couldn't still be letting that humiliating episode in her past affect her behaviour.

Could she?

'One look in the mirror,' she said crisply, 'is enough to tell me I'm not beautiful.'

'There is a beauty in character, but if you don't believe that, then surely you'll admit that skin as fine and translucent as silk, and eyes the colour of a summer sky at midnight, and aristocratic bones, a mouth that's soft and provocative, are every bit as powerfully attractive and exciting as the attributes of a woman who conforms by the exact centimetre to the current standards.' His voice was cool and impersonal, so that it took her a moment to realise that he was speaking of her.

When she did, she was almost suffocated by the swift heated response that flared through her.

Oh, God, she thought distractedly, I have to get out of here!

He picked up her hand and ran his thumb over her palm and fingers. 'Yes,' he said, smiling oddly, his great height dwarfing her. 'Long fingers with the signs of hard work on them. They have their own sort of beauty, too.'

She remembered those same signs on his hands, remembered only too well the sensations that had exploded through her when he touched her breasts, her thighs. Need—lying, dangerous need, sweet and thick as honey—poured through her. Mingled with the exhalations of the roses she could smell the warm, slightly musky male scent which had haunted her dreams for the past year. A shiver that had nothing to do with the temperature pulled the tiny hairs on her skin upright.

Into the charged silence she said huskily, 'Cooks get calluses, just as station owners do.' And because he showed no signs of releasing her, she muttered, 'I'm getting cold—I'd better go in. Goodnight, Nick.'

It was retreat, pure and simple, but she fled up the steps and into the house without caring. Much more of that, she thought as she scampered up the stairs, and she'd have melted in a puddle at his feet.

He didn't come up until about an hour afterwards. What had he been thinking of out there under the moon?

Mimicking sleep, she breathed evenly in and out, conscientiously checking the movements of her diaphragm. Sleep eluded her. Over and over in her mind she replayed the scene down by the pool. What had he been doing? Why had he behaved so—so——? She searched for the right word and failed to find it.

He had known what he was doing; he had deliberately told her she was beautiful, he had deliberately held her hand in his big warm one, he had looked significantly at her, not because he believed what he was saying, but for some ulterior reason.

Perhaps he had been punishing her for running away from Spanish Castle.

She burrowed her hot face into the pillow. Hardly. Why should he? If she had meant anything to him at all, he'd have contacted her.

If only he knew, she had been punished enough for her stupidity. Scarcely a night went past that she didn't recall those maddened minutes in his arms; even now, she felt the rapid quickening of response in her body and the breath shortening in her lungs.

And anyway, he had seduced her, so, if anyone wanted to punish anyone, she was the injured party! Firmly repressing various wanton methods of punishment that floated from some wicked part of her unconscious, she decided she wasn't ever going to know why he had orchestrated that scene out in the moonlight, so she wasn't going to worry about it. From now on, she would just make sure she stayed out of his way.

Especially in moonlight, with summer jasmine and roses and lavender lending their own particular sorcery to the atmosphere.

It shouldn't be too difficult, she thought as at last blessed sleep hazed her mind. He lived at Spanish Castle and she had no intention of going there again.

He swam at dawn. After some minutes spent listening to the sounds of his progress through the water, Minerva crept out of bed and across to the window, keeping to one side so that he couldn't see her. Craning her head, she peered out. The rising sun gilded a water-darkened head, wide shoulders and long arms; a thin gloss of water revealed muscles that flexed and coiled as he powered the length of the pool.

Minerva took a deep breath and turned swiftly away, the sight of him filling her eyes, her head, making her dizzy even after she sat down on the side of the bed. He looked like some huntsman in the age of dawn, unashamed of his masculinity, revelling in his physical perfection. A shudder wreaked dangerous enchantment through her.

Closing her hand into a fist, she kept it clenched until the knuckles turned white. She would not let this useless, unbidden hunger destroy her peace.

Yet she couldn't quench the perilous flicker of anticipation that brought a glow to her white skin and a glint of excitement to her eyes.

She was eating breakfast out on the terrace with Ruth when he came down dressed in casual trousers and a polo shirt that gave a slight blue tinge to the silvery radiance of his eyes.

'Darling,' Ruth beamed, kissing him as he bent to her. 'How lovely to see you. So you enjoyed last night.'

'It was interesting,' he admitted, looking directly across the table to Minerva. 'Good morning, Minerva. You're looking a little more formal than when I saw you last.'

With elevated eyebrows Ruth looked from one to another.

'I went for a swim after I got home,' Minerva explained hastily. 'Nick appeared just as I got out, so he saw me dripping wet and wrapped in a towel.'

'We used to always wear caps,' Ruth said, pouring him a cup of coffee. 'It was much better for our hair than getting it wet all the time. When are you going back, Nick?'

'Today, I'm afraid. I'm off as soon as I've eaten.'

'Oh, such a short visit!' Ruth looked sadly at him, then brightened. Her eyes twinkled. 'Never mind, we'll be seeing you in a week's time.'

'Do you want to fly, or will you come up by road?'

Minerva looked up sharply from her cereal to find Nick regarding her with an impassivity too bland to be genuine. She switched her gaze to Ruth, who was sipping tea and looking complacent. 'Are you going to Spanish Castle?' she blurted.

'We all are, darling, haven't I told you? We're spending Christmas there.' Apparently unaware of Minerva's dismay, Ruth smiled at the man who was eating a large plate of sausages with smoked oysters. 'I'm so looking forward to it. Nick, isn't breakfast lovely? Minerva made it for us.'

'It's superb,' he said.

He knew, Minerva thought dazedly; he understood her horror at the prospect of Christmas spent at his home. His eyes gleamed with unkind amusement as he said, 'But you're not having any?'

She shrugged, managing to appear as composed as he was. She didn't know exactly what was going on, but she recognised that look of Ruth's. 'I haven't changed. I'm still a toast and cereal person.'

'A pity,' he said casually. 'Do you have to watch your weight? Surely that's an occupational hazard for cooks?'

She shook her head. 'I seem to have inherited my mother's genes. She was a racehorse, I believe.'

'And your father can eat anything and everything and never puts an ounce on.' Ruth looked ruefully down at her plumpish self. 'Whereas I have to be so careful. Stella was the same.'

She spoke unaffectedly of her daughter, with none of the anguish that had abraded her voice a year ago. At least they had all been able to come to terms with the tragedy of Stella's life and death.

An hour later, when Nick had been carried off by taxi to the airport, Minerva asked casually, 'How long do you plan to stay at Spanish Castle?'

'Oh, for about three weeks.' Ruth bustled around, putting the dishes on to a wagon. 'No, darling, don't you do that! You know it's a rule that when you come home you do nothing. It was really rather naughty of you to cook breakfast this morning, but perhaps you wanted to?' For a special reason, her tone implied as she smiled archly at Minerva.

Had she? She said composedly, 'Not really. I just saw the oysters. My last employer loved them.' She hesitated, then said, 'Perhaps I could do some cooking while we're up at Spanish Castle? Nick's housekeeper might like to have Christmas off this year. Is it still Helen Borrows?'

'Yes, and I doubt whether Nick would approve of you working for nothing,' Ruth said serenely. 'After all, you've already helped him out once. Darling, what are you planning to do today?'

Minerva looked out at the sunlight gleaming on the gardens, gilding the white and pastel flowers. 'I think I might just loll about,' she said, despising herself because she knew she was going to spend the day analysing every second since her first glimpse of Nick last night.

'What a good idea. Don't forget the party tonight.'

It was the usual run-up to Christmas, busy, hot, crammed with engagements. The dinner with other old girls had told everyone that she was home, so that now she had more invitations than she could hope to deal with. More than she wanted to deal with, come to that. Minerva was not the most social of people.

Nevertheless, her progress from party to barbecue to a day on someone's yacht and then to an extravaganza at a racecourse helped her forget that, inexorably, her return to Spanish Castle was coming closer and closer.

CHAPTER SEVEN

BECAUSE Ruth decided they had too much luggage to put in Nick's Cessna, they drove up by car. She had a raft of little phobias, and flying was not her favourite way to travel, even when Nick piloted the plane. Besides, the middle of haymaking was an awkward time for him to take a day off.

Travelling north took them a long, hot morning along traffic-clogged roads past magnificent seascapes, between hills that were blue-green with remnants of native bush and plantations of Montery pines, past dairy farms and kiwi-fruit and citrus orchards, and sheep and cattle farms where new and unusual breeds grazed under the intense northern sun.

South of Kerikeri they left the main highway for the secondary road that led up to the coast; after thirty or so kilometres they turned off again and began the winding ascent towards the *kauri* forest and Spanish Castle.

'It's an amazing place, isn't it?' Brian took a corner slightly too fast. Gravel spat from the wheels as the car planed sideways. Fortunately the road was empty of traffic. He dealt efficiently with the skid before giving a slight, penitent grin at Ruth's automatic command to take care.

'Sorry,' he said, 'it takes me a little while to get used to gravel roads. Just as well Nick didn't see that. He has very rigid standards when it comes to driving. Last Christmas when Kane skidded around a corner he grounded him for a week. If I'd done it Kane would

138

have been resentful, but he accepted Nick's decision without a murmur.'

'Hero worship.' Minerva's voice sounded just right; amused, light, splendidly offhand.

'Oh, yes. Not that Kane would admit it, of course. And, for all that Nick's as hard as nails, he couldn't have a better man to look up to.'

'Kane worked for him last Christmas holidays,' Ruth said. She sighed. 'This will be our first Christmas without Kane. I'm going to miss him badly.

'You'll be able to talk to him,' Minerva said gently. 'And think of the fun when he comes home! It's only a few more weeks now.'

'Talking on the phone's not the same, but I wouldn't stand in his way, not for anything. And it was the right decision—he's having a wonderful time.' Ruth relapsed into gentle melancholy for several moments before cheering up. 'I'm glad we're going to be at Spanish Castle. Nick is a darling, and Christmas here will be magnificent.'

Minerva thought bleakly that there was something about Nick, and Spanish Castle, that was larger than life. The first Peveril, the man who had looked at a pile of volcanic rocks and seen a castle in Spain, the man who had stolen another man's wife and in the end was left with nothing but memories and the son of that liaison, must have been like Nick.

For all his worldliness and his great wealth and style, she could imagine him as a pirate, taking a woman if there was no other way. Beneath his urbane exterior there was definitely a streak of the primitive.

Although she couldn't see him letting a woman he loved go back to a husband who didn't value her. Wondering just why the first Nicholas's love had left him, Minerva tried to avoid thinking about the man who was waiting ahead.

The next three weeks promised to be a time of considerable tension. The year she had spent away had altered Nick in some indefinable way, and she was wary of the change. And if Genevieve Chatswood was around much, it was going to take all of Minerva's strength of character to behave in a normal, serene manner.

Smoothing the scowl from her face she said suddenly, 'There it is.'

Her father pulled to the side of the road and stopped the car. 'Impressive, isn't it?'

Minerva's eyes drifted from the huge crags on the skyline to the house at the base, white as a pearl in its gardens, sheltered by the loving embrace of the trees but open to the brilliant panorama of sea and sky in the north and east.

No wonder Nick was the way he was!

They resumed their sedate progress through bush that was cool and echoing with the shrill sound of cicadas, past the signpost where Nick had materialised out of the mist, and down the road towards the stone pillars.

Minerva had first seen Spanish Castle in spring, surrounded by magnolias and cherries, the gardens gay with daffodils and freesias and the regal scarlet and purples of babianas and sparaxias, daphne perfuming the air and daisies and mock orange blooming rampantly between the roses.

Now it was summer, and the only magnolia flowering was a huge grandiflora that held big white lemon-perfumed cups to the blazing sky. Although the gardens were as colourful, the roses as sweet, the prevailing scent was that of the hay being made in three big paddocks close by the house.

It was even more beautiful. Northland was summer country, looking its best under a brazen sun and skies as blue as the robes of a medieval madonna. Minerva gazed eagerly about as they drove through the pillars and along the drive towards the house, pulling to a halt with a flourish just as Helen Borrows came through the front door.

Ruth's heartfelt groan of relief as she unfolded herself from the front seat brought a twinkle to the housekeeper's eye.

'How was the trip up?' she said. 'Nick's sorry he's not here to greet you himself, but they need to get the hay in as soon as possible so he won't be back until just before dinnertime. I'll show you your rooms now, and when you've tidied up we'll have a cup of tea.'

The homestead was the same, cool now instead of warm, and with the same faint, evocative aroma of beeswax and lavender, and the same perfume of flowers. It was like coming home.

But Minerva had to bite back a protest as she walked into her room. It was the one she had had a year ago, too close to Nick's. Stella's room. Except that nothing of her stepsister lingered there, or anywhere else at Spanish Castle.

On the dressing table a silver bowl of roses glowed like transformed flames. Eyes misting, Minerva bent to smell them before dumping her pack on to the chair by the desk.

Five minutes later she'd washed the dust from her face and bare arms in the bathroom, and was revelling in the cool, clean feeling. As she brushed her hair into satiny submission an uncomfortable anticipation coiled itself around her heart, at once frightening and shaming and exciting.

Nick came in when the sun was almost on the horizon. Minerva was lying on a lounger under the spreading canes of wistaria, eyes almost closed, fingers stroking through Penelope's thick fur.

Before she heard him, and certainly before the sleeping cat stirred, she sensed his presence. Her hand stilled; it took her a moment to summon the courage to look up, and even then she veiled that first glance with her lashes.

He stepped from the thick shade of the sheltering trees and came across the lawn with a lean-hipped stride, shirt slung across one gleaming copper shoulder, hat pushed back on to his head, shorts and legs patterned with green flecks of grass.

His face was dark and streaked with sweat, as were his arms and chest, the work-wrought muscles outlined by the sheen of moisture. He looked very big, and the smile that showed white against the hard angles of his face was confident and ironic.

Minerva asked jerkily, 'Have you finished?'

'Broken the back of it, but the contractors will be working until the dew comes down.'

'When did you start?'

'Dawn.'

'You must be exhausted. Can I get you a drink? There's some orange juice and a spare glass here.' Don't fuss, she told herself.

'I could probably drink Cook Strait dry.'

She poured juice and handed it over, watching the muscles move in his throat as he drank. Fierce and dangerous, need sapped the strength from her bones.

'You look as cool and fresh as spring,' he said, setting the glass down, his narrowed gaze raking her supine length.

Minerva felt that regard in every cell. A delicious lassitude sapped her of resistance; he looked at her with a pirate's acquisitive eye, as though she was his for the taking. And instead of resenting it she felt herself preen, her body react in a thousand unseen ways to the bold speculation in his glance.

With a clipped intonation he said, 'I'll go and shower.'

Unable to trust her voice, Minerva nodded.

'See you later, then,' he said.

Once he had gone she dragged a deep breath into lungs starved of air. 'You might have warned me,' she told the recumbent and totally uninterested Penelope.

The cat yawned pinkly, stretched and yawned again, before springing on to the veranda and setting off down the steps towards a certain spot in a nest of brilliant blue lobelias that caught the rays of the setting sun.

Trying to calm her racing heart, Minerva rolled over on to her side and stared fixedly at the cheerful faces of a mass of blue pansies. She had organised herself for his appearance. She had known just how she was going to behave; with dignity and grace and a cool, unshatterable composure. She'd been ready.

And then he'd come upon her like that, and the defences she had so carefully erected had crumbled like mud-brick in a cloudburst.

It simply wasn't fair!

Her body wasn't co-operating, either. She might be obsessed with the man physically, but there was no need to display her weakness to Nick's pale, perceptive eyes.

Fortunately when he arrived back, properly clothed in one of his handmade cotton shirts and a pair of trousers cut to show heavily muscled thighs and calves and the alarming length of both, he had Ruth with him.

So things were a little easier, but there was enough strain in the lazy air for Minerva to go in to dinner with her nerves jumping. How on earth was she going to last out the three weeks she'd have to stay before she could decently leave?

Over an excellent meal she suggested that perhaps Helen might like to spend more of the holiday season with her family; if so, she said lightly, looking Nick straight in the eye, she'd be very happy to take over the cooking until she left. 'Christmas Day, too,' she finished, prickling at the subtle mockery of Nick's smile.

'Of course, if you'd like to do it,' he said. 'But we have to all help.'

There was a chorus of agreement. Helen was delighted, and so it was settled.

Tomorrow, Minerva planned as she tried to sleep in her quiet bedroom several hours later, she would ask the housekeeper what preparations she had made. She lay for some time mentally preparing a superb meal, the sort that would knock everyone's socks off.

Who are you trying to fool? she demanded. You don't care about anyone else, it's Nick you want to impress.

She closed her eyes. Stella's face and curvy little form danced against the darkness. As soon as Minerva had grown old enough to realise that envy was useless, she had stopped longing for the unattainable, and it hurt to do it now. She knew why, of course. Just once she'd like to see that familiar sensual glow of interest in some man's eyes when he looked at her.

Some man! It was Nick's eyes she wanted to dazzle, Nick's heart she wanted to subjugate.

She winced. Coming here—for all that she felt a powerful familiarity, almost possessiveness, as though she was coming home—had been the biggest mistake she had made since deciding to visit Spanish Castle the previous year.

If she forced herself to face facts, it was very simple, really. She had loved Nick the minute she saw him, she loved him now, and she would love him until she died.

What a joke! Because she knew damned well he didn't feel the same. Even if he did want to make love to her, there was a barrier, transparent as his eyes yet impossible to break through. He had retired his emotions behind a wall of ice.

Or perhaps she was just being foolish. Perhaps when he looked at Genevieve his glance was clear and candid.

At least the woman wasn't going to be around for two of Minerva's three weeks in purgatory. Over dinner Ruth had asked where she was and if she'd be there for Christmas, her artless interest robbing the question of offence.

Nick had raised his brows and managed to look both surprised and amused at once. 'No, she's spending the holidays with her family,' he answered calmly.

Turning her head, Minerva gazed blindly at the ornate cornice of the ceiling. Exhausted though she was, she wanted to get up and banish this fever from her blood with hard running, or riding, or swimming.

Eventually, the quietness, the deep serenity, calmed her racing heart, but she still couldn't sleep. The morepork in the shelter belt was having a night off, for no call of 'morepork! morepork!' echoed across the lawn. No soft breath of breeze echoed in her ears, nothing could be heard but the immense silence of the night.

She hadn't pulled the curtains, and for hours she lay watching the slow, inexorable dance of the stars through the window, Orion the mighty hunter of summer striding across his kingdom as Nick had come across the lawn towards her...

Sighing, she yanked the pillow over her head and finally found oblivion.

Next morning she woke to the sound of the hay-makers' tractors and machinery, muffled by the shelter belt but omnipresent. Through the open window the air poured, clean and crisp and damp; Minerva padded across and stayed there for some minutes looking out at the dew-fresh, sunlit garden.

In the crystal light of morning her conviction the night before that she was a captive for life seemed ridiculously melodramatic. One day, she thought as she turned away from the window, one day she'd look back on today and smile rather pityingly for the anguish she was enduring. One day she'd exorcise Nick from her life neatly and irrevocably.

It was a beautiful place to spend purgatory in. Nick would be spending most of his time out on the station, which would leave her to cope with his overpowering

presence and her own wildfire reactions only at meal-
times and the evenings. She'd manage.

And when it was over she'd stay away. Sooner or later
this wholly inopportune passion would die of star-
vation, just as her desire for Paul had.

Over breakfast Nick asked if she'd like to go into
Kerikeri with him.

'What a good idea,' Ruth said before she could answer,
leaning forward. 'I want some moisturiser from the
chemist. I can't think how I managed to, but I left mine
behind.'

'Are you coming?' Minerva asked hopefully.

Ruth settled back into her chair, looking remarkably
complacent. 'No, thank you, darling. I must be getting
old—I was quite stiff when I got out of the car yesterday. I'm not moving today, I'm just going to lie about
with a book and a cold drink.'

Brian decided that he too would lie about in the shade.
And Minerva had no excuse, no reason for not going
into Kerikeri with Nick.

Aloud, she said, 'OK. When do you want to go?'

'At ten,' he said, and turned to other things.

After breakfast Minerva went in search of Helen to
see what menu she had organised for Christmas dinner.
While Nick was doing whatever he wanted to in Kerikeri,
she'd buy what was necessary for any changes or ad-
ditions she decided on.

Helen was bubbling with pleasure. 'It will be the first
time I've had a whole Christmas Day to myself for years,'
she volunteered, adding with a smile, 'and I think it
might be an important day for us. Our son's working in
Pakistan and he's bringing a girl back with him, an
English nurse. He hasn't said anything, but I'm sure
they're thinking of getting married. About time, too!
And my daughter from Christchurch—remember, I had
to go down to be with her when you were here last?—

well, she and her husband and the baby will be here as well.'

She had stuck to the conventional with her menu, planning to serve the usual roast turkey dinner and plum duff; Minerva decided to provide lighter dishes as well as the traditional ones. Ruth adored the idea of a traditional blockbuster Christmas dinner, but her appetite needed tempting, especially if the day was hot.

Obediently following the housekeeper around the pantry and chiller room with its stacks of frozen foodstuffs from the farm, Minerva made mental notes. She wasn't going to need much extra. The vegetables and strawberries were already ordered from local growers, Helen told her, and would be picked up on Christmas Eve.

By the time this was done she had to rush into a thin cotton shirt and trousers in her favourite blue to be ready by ten. Nick, one of whose faults was a maddening punctuality, had the car out when Minerva arrived, slightly breathless, her hair floating around her face in an ash-brown cloud instead of imprisoned in its usual neat knot. Settling in the front seat, she kept her gaze firmly ahead.

She half expected some comment, but after an amused glance at the fine, flyaway mass Nick began to discuss the latest political scandal. Slowly, she relaxed. She had forgotten, she thought halfway to Kerikeri, just how intelligent and unbiased he was, how far from the die-hard conservative one always expected landowners to be. Without thinking, she said so.

'Why?' he asked mildly.

She shrugged. 'Oh, farmers have the reputation of being reactionary.'

His smile was tolerant. 'Perhaps someone has to be conservative so that the airy-fairy liberals won't float off the face of the earth. Farmers and people who make their living from working with nature tend not to have much time for theories. They've seen too many of them shot down in flames by a dose of reality.'

'Are you a cynic?'

The wide shoulders moved. 'I don't think so. Cynical, perhaps, but not completely lost to idealism.

A lamb shot across the road in front of them. Instantly Nick stopped the car. The lamb came equipped with its mother, who stood belligerently on the low bank and faced them down, stamping one front hoof as she dared them to come closer.

'We'll have to put them back,' Nick said, unclipping his seatbelt. 'Open that gate, will you, and stand at the end of it? Be ready to leap out on to the road and head them off if they try to escape, which they will. That's a toey old ewe there.'

He was right. Neither lamb nor ewe wanted to return to the paddock. By the time they'd managed to coax them through the gate, Minerva was eyeing both uncooperative and thoroughly irritating animals with a thought to converting them into roasts.

The little episode, insignificant though it was, gave her a new angle on Nick's enigmatic personality. Even when the ewe and her lamb had been utterly infuriating, he had been patient. As well, he had taken the time to stop and put them back.

Wondering why she should be surprised, Minerva realised with a little spasm of shame that her view of him as the aloof, dark lord of the manor had become completely entrenched.

'I went out to see Rusty this morning,' she said. 'If I didn't know it was impossible, I'd say he recognised me. He certainly seemed pleased to see me.'

'Why is it so impossible?'

'Well, it's been a year.'

'Dogs remember for much longer than that. Anyway, why would he forget someone who made a habit of giving him the tastiest leftovers?' He was smiling.

'I didn't know you knew.'

He directed a swift, slanted glance her way. 'I noticed everything,' he said calmly, a remark which left her speechless.

Kerikeri was bustling. Tourists and holidaymakers, as well as the local farmers and orchardists, were all gearing up for Christmas. The schools were out so the streets buzzed with children, all seething with the unsuppressed excitement that only the prospect of presents and feasting and summer holidays could elicit.

After handing over a key to the car and arranging to meet her in half an hour, Nick strode off through the crowds like—well, Minerva thought, hiding a wry smile as she made her way to the nearest supermarket, like the lord of the manor.

Twenty minutes later she had bought most of the things she needed to make sure he never forgot this Christmas dinner. She deposited the bags in the car, but the prospect of sitting in the heat while she waited for Nick didn't appeal at all. However, when she looked along the street she saw Nick's tall figure coming through the crowds.

Wistfully, she watched as people smiled at him and nodded to him and stopped to exchange a few words. Perhaps her mother's early death had left her basically insecure; this was something she had never experienced, this confidence, this sense of home. If she belonged to Nick, she thought painfully, if he belonged to her, she would never again have to search for it. He would be enough for her.

'I hope you haven't waited long,' he said as he came up.

Her hair was warm and heavy against her neck and shoulders as she shook her head. 'No, I've just got here.'

'Good,' he said, smiling and opening the car door for her.

That smile did such strange things to her that she didn't notice where they were going until her eyes were caught by a dazzle of sun on water. 'This isn't the way home, is it?'

'I want to see friends down the Inlet. Do you mind?'

'No, of course not.' But she did.

'You'll like them,' he promised.

They lived down the Inlet in a huge stained wooden house with its own private beach, and a garden that was even more lush and riotous than the one at Spanish Castle. Tegan and Kieran Sinclair and their two delightful daughters of three and one were up from Auckland for the holidays. An older son, Minerva discovered, was coming up the following day with his grandparents.

They were curious, although they hid it well. Obviously old friends of Nick's, they greeted him with the easy camaraderie that had to be forged over a number of years.

Tegan was fun, and her tall, extremely handsome, rather severe merchant banker husband was clearly as much in love with her as she was with him. For the first time Minerva saw Nick with close friends; he was too reserved to reveal much of his thoughts and emotions, but in the Sinclairs' home there was a subtle aura of relaxation about him she'd never seen before.

How much psychic energy he must use to keep up that front!

Except that it wasn't really a front. Authority was as much a part of him as the cool grey eyes and the proudly held head. It was just that most people never got past the outward mask; they took the effortless, disciplined strength, the persona he presented to the world, to be the whole man. Nick was not vulnerable, but he had areas of vulnerability in him that he protected with a frightening fierceness.

In some ways Minerva understood him very well, knew far more about him than even these friends of long standing. In others she didn't understand him at all.

Lucy, the older daughter, a puppy-like little creature with flaxen hair and a wide, happy grin, left her sand-castle to wander up to where the adults were sitting in the shade of a huge *pohutukawa* tree. With the confidence of a child who knew she was loved and privileged, she climbed into Nick's lap and gazed adoringly up into his face. At the first available opportunity she announced to Minerva, 'Uncle Nick is my godfather. Not Emma's and not Ross's.'

Not yours, her tone implied. Minerva said, 'He's a very lucky man.'

Lucy giggled. 'He brings us presents.' Her gaze wandered towards the bedroom where an interesting stack of parcels delivered by Nick had been stashed by her mother.

'Those are for Christmas,' Tegan said sternly.

Nick grinned, his expression softening marvellously, and flicked his god-daughter's straight little nose with its five charming freckles. 'Wait until Christmas Day,' he said.

'Five more sleeps,' Lucy said gloomily, but she gave him a swift hug before sliding down on to the quarry tiles of the terrace.

Her mother waited until she had joined her sister on the beach a few feet away before saying, 'You indulge them, Nick.'

'I like them,' he said simply, half closing his eyes against a probing ray of sunlight.

Kieran laughed. 'We do, too. But no more musical instruments. After you gave Lucy that drum for her birthday she woke us every morning at five with a tattoo. It took us months to convince her we like to sleep a little longer.'

'She still takes it to bed with her,' Tegan added, not trying to hide the doting note in her voice.

Nick's lashes curled, thick and dark, against his skin. 'All right,' he said peacefully. 'No more drums.'

Minerva's heart stood still. All she wanted, all her happiness and her future, was bound up in this man. For the first time she accepted fully, with her mind as well as her heart, just how bleak and destitute her life was going to be without him. It was a shattering realisation, and to her astonishment her predominant emotion was a violent resentment.

Common sense dispersed most of that, but enough lingered to keep her quiet for the rest of the visit.

On the way home he observed with a hint of steel, 'I gather you didn't like them.'

Indignation chilled her voice. 'You're wrong, I liked them very much.'

His dark eyebrows lifted. 'I'm glad. Kieran is one of my oldest friends. And Tegan is a delight.'

Agreeing, Minerva wondered why he had taken her down to meet them. He could quite easily have delivered the presents by himself. It wasn't likely that he simply enjoyed her company and wanted to see more of her. Things were rarely so simple with Nick.

It could have been just a kind gesture, introducing her to his friends. He was kind; she had known that from that first day at Spanish Castle when he had comforted Helen Borrows so unaffectedly. He'd been kind to Ruth, to little Lucy; when he spoke to every other woman of his acquaintance, she thought savagely, it was with affection in his voice.

When he spoke to Minerva there was nothing but cool control.

Yet he had wanted her once.

Wanting, of course, was lust, not love. Perhaps his ability to love had died with Stella.

The instant he had loomed out of the rain and the mist on Silver Demon something basic and inexorable had happened to Minerva; some inner, unknown rampart had melted away and left her exposed to the force-field of his magnetism.

Would it have happened if Stella had been waiting at Spanish Castle for her?

She didn't know. She would never know. It was a raw irony that she was now as much Nick's as his dog and his horse, as Spanish Castle itself, yet because Stella had died so wretchedly there was no future for either of them. She still couldn't grab a chance at a happiness that would be fundamentally flawed by Stella's misery.

'That's a grim look,' he said. 'What are you thinking?'

She looked at him, and something in her face must have told him for he said harshly, 'Stella. I wonder if she knew that killing herself was the one way to become immortal.'

'I doubt it,' she answered quietly, her heart aching. 'She wasn't thinking at all clearly, poor Stella.'

'Neither of us was.' His jaw tightened. 'At least we know what was the matter with her.'

'Yes.'

'I wish to God,' he said savagely, 'that I'd met her father. Just once.'

Minerva flinched, devoutly thankful that the man was dead. It was very easy to imagine Nick taking vengeance on a man who had wronged a child so hideously. Apart from the personal aspect, he had an easy manner with the little Sinclair girls that revealed his liking for children.

'How's Frank?' she asked.

He flicked a sideways glance at her. 'He's fine. His wife has settled in Kerikeri so he sees his children whenever he wants to, and I think there's another romance in the offing. He's off the booze. And Jillian and John Howard have bought their own farm on the road between Helensville and Wellsford. They seem to be well settled.'

'Good.' For a reason she wasn't prepared to examine too closely Minerva was glad the Howards had gone.

Spanish Castle lay drowsily under the sun, the newly cut paddocks bare and yellow, great round bales of hay piled under cover. As they drove through the gateposts a small caravan of the contractor's machinery came towards them. Nick pulled over on to the grass and let them past, talking for a while to the man through the car window.

Minerva sat quietly. The contractor spoke to him as one who knew him well, but there was respect in his voice. When he left he wished them a Merry Christmas and drove off through the gates.

'I suppose he's hoping those clouds don't come to anything.' Minerva nodded at the white galleons building up on the eastern horizon.

'There's no rain in that lot. A stationary anticyclone extends all the way up to the tradewinds and right across the Tasman Sea to Australia,' Nick said. 'A small tropical storm bumbling around near New Caledonia might give us a wet Christmas, but even if it does head down this way it'll be at least three days before it gets here.'

'I'd like to be able to read the weather,' she said dreamily. 'When I was on the yacht I envied the sailors. They used to be able to tell what was going to happen sometimes several weeks ahead.'

His hard mouth was not softened by a slashing grin. 'They were probably like me, used the long-range weather forecasts.'

Minerva laughed. 'They probably did, the liars. But I thought farmers could read weather signs.'

'Most of us can read clouds reasonably well, but that's short-term stuff. If we were able to be more accurate with long-term predictions we wouldn't lose stock in floods and droughts, and we'd know exactly when to cut the hay,' he said, driving around the back of the home-stead to the garage. 'Don't you carry all that stuff in; I'll give you a hand.'

The next few days passed slowly in an odd, watchful tranquillity. Minerva's hungry heart took what small comfort she could from Nick's presence.

In the evenings there were parties of various sorts, a large barbecue for all the staff a week before Christmas, and several road parties, most extremely informal. Inconspicuously, Minerva watched Nick, wondering why he seemed to be playing a part. Oh, he talked and laughed and joined in; he was an extremely welcome guest, as skilled at that as he was at being a host. Yet there was an isolation about him that made her wonder just how much he enjoyed socialising.

At the Sinclairs' he had been completely relaxed. He was just as relaxed with Ruth and Brian. A very private man, he apparently had a few very close friends, and, apart from a gaggle of distant cousins and his mother in Singapore, only Stella's family to call his own.

Nobody else appeared to recognise this aspect of his character. Popular as he was, his neighbours treated him with liking and respect, and sometimes a hint of awe. Women, Minerva noted acidly, did everything but swoon in front of him to catch his attention, but neither neigh-bours nor hopeful women looked far beneath the surface.

Several nights before Christmas he asked her if she'd like to go with him to a drinks party in Kerikeri. Minerva said no, thank you, she thought she'd have an early night, and he nodded, his cool, pure grey eyes lingering a moment on her averted face. Her refusal clearly didn't upset him in the least.

She went to bed at her normal time, but she was reading when Ruth's knock on the door sounded above the gently falling rain outside. Nick's long-range weather forecaster had been right; the tropical storm had hit right on time. Not that it was a storm now, merely a patch of rain that should be well past Northland by Christmas Day.

Minerva looked enquiringly at her stepmother as she came into the room, wondering whether she had come for comfort. Kane's absence was still giving Ruth melancholy moments, but this didn't seem to be one of them.

'Hello, darling, still awake?' she asked blithely.

'Yes.' Minerva wasn't going to tell her stepmother that she wouldn't sleep until Nick came home.

Holding her magazine up to conceal a smile, she watched the older woman fidget around the room for a few minutes. Ruth was transparent; she had something to say, and she wasn't sure how to bring it up, but she'd find a way.

'Is everything organised for Christmas Day?' Ruth asked.

'Yes. Totally under control.'

Ruth twitched the curtain closed, then wandered across to the dressing table. 'Didn't you want to go out tonight?' she murmured casually, setting Minerva's bottle of Dune perfume down with a sharp little crack.

Minerva's brows drew together, but she answered readily enough, 'No, not tonight.' She couldn't stand another evening of seeing women make idiots of themselves over Nick, but she wasn't going to tell Ruth that, either.

'Do you like Nick?'

Minerva closed her magazine and put it on the bedside table. The little movement gave the quick colour in her face a chance to subside. 'Yes,' she said composedly, 'I do.'

'Oh. That's good. Why didn't you want to go out with him tonight?'

The suspicion that the first question had given rise to changed to certainty. 'Ruth,' she asked incredulously, 'are you matchmaking?'

Ruth flushed but said firmly, 'Well, what if I am? It's time you settled down, darling, and Nick is—well, I don't need to tell you what he is.'

'What he is, is Stella's widower,' Minerva said brutally.

Ruth's face crumpled. 'Stella's been dead for over two years, darling. We can't live in the past. We'll never forget her, but it's time we moved on.'

'Ruth, Nick and I are not in love.' Each word hurt, but they had to be said.

Ruth sat down on the end of the bed and looked at her stepdaughter with an unwavering regard. 'He's interested,' she said quickly.

Minerva's heart gave a great bound. Before she could stop herself she demanded grittily, 'How do you know?'

'Don't look like that! It's all right, I haven't discussed you with him, not at all, but I know when a man's attracted, and he is, I'm certain. He watches you——'

Minerva leaned back against the pillow, forcing her expression to remain unchanged. 'Perhaps he does,' she said lightly. 'I'm the only woman here who's anywhere near his age. Nick's not in love with me, Ruth. Don't go making things awkward for both of us by pushing us together. We're well content with things as they are.'

Which was a lie, of course. Nick might have been well content, but she was not. However, her blood ran cold at the prospect of Ruth matchmaking.

So she finished with a firmness that bordered on severity, 'If he's interested in anyone, it's probably Genevieve. Only a couple of weeks ago you were saying you thought they'd eventually get married.'

On a rueful note Ruth explained, 'I was trying to make you jealous.'

Minerva sighed. 'Oh, Ruth,' she said gently.

'Well, I know you—you're attracted, and you'd be perfect for him.' She bit her lip. 'He needs someone who will love him, and you've always been good at that.'

Minerva smiled, her heart cracking quietly. 'I need someone to love me, too,' she said.

'I—see.' Ruth directed one of her disconcertingly shrewd glances at her stepdaughter. After a moment she gave Minerva a swift hug and got to her feet. 'All right then, I'm sorry if I hurt you. No more games. I'll be good. Sleep well, darling.'

When she had gone Minerva lay awake listening to the persistent downpour. Eventually, after Nick's headlights split through the vertical sheets of rain, she turned over and went to sleep.

CHAPTER EIGHT

MINERVA woke to a wet morning. There had been heavy showers during the night, but now rain fell gently, inexorably, beading the plants and trees with crystals, collecting in tiny silver pools across the green lawn.

After breakfast Nick and Brian played several cutthroat games of billiards while Minerva browsed through a turn-of-the-century recipe book she had found in the library. Ruth sat under one of the green-shaded lamps doing exquisite *petit point*.

'One of these days,' Brian said resignedly at the end of the game, 'I'll beat you.'

Nick grinned. 'Not this morning, though. I have to do some work.'

He left the room. Brian settled down to read the newspaper. Minerva looked sightlessly at the recipe book in her lap.

Shortly afterwards she decided to bake a large batch of Afghan biscuits, and had just walked into the kitchen when Nick stopped in the doorway.

'Do you want to come for a ride?' he asked casually.

'Where are you going?'

'I feel like some fresh air, but my excuse is that I need to check the creek. We could go and see the waterfall; it should look good after last night's rain.'

Minerva cast a glance through the window. The rain had almost stopped, but the drizzle was Northland heavy, extremely wetting. Still, she'd never seen the waterfall, where the creek that drained the crags hurtled over the cliff and on to the homestead plateau.

'There's some of my mother's wet weather gear in the mud-room that should fit you,' he said.

'All right,' Minerva said. 'I'll get changed.'

Five minutes later she arrived at the door of the mud-room clad in jeans and a cotton T-shirt. Nick looked her over with an open and complete interest that made the blood pump feverishly through her veins. He'd already pulled on an oiled cotton riding coat that would keep him completely dry while he was on Demon, the one he'd been wearing the day he'd appeared out of the mist.

Ruth's words from the night before jingled in her ears. *'He's interested'*. Minerva wasn't interested in 'interested'. The year away had made her greedy; she wanted so much more than a practical marriage. She wanted love and commitment and passion and a lifetime.

Fat chance!

Doing her best to ignore that frankly sensual survey, she shrugged into the coat he held out and moved away to pull on gumboots.

'Do you think the horses will forgive us?' she said too brightly. 'I don't suppose they like being worked in the rain.'

'Demon's ready for anything, and Mixed Biscuits is so placid she wouldn't care if you took her out in an earthquake.'

They left twenty minutes later, riding through a downpour that was probably the final effort of the depression. Halfway across the first paddock Nick gave her a grin that was pure pleasure. Her spirits rose, sending delicate colour into her cheeks, a gleam of delight to her eyes.

'No Rusty?' she shouted.

He shook his head.

Minerva urged Mixed Biscuits, a charming piebald mare, closer to Demon. 'I never thought I'd see the day when a farmer rides out without his dog.'

'He'd just be a damned nuisance.'

But they hadn't gone more than a kilometre from the homestead when Rusty caught them up, grinning, yet making it obvious by his submissive demeanour that he knew he was in the wrong.

Minerva laughed. 'Did someone let him off?'

'It looks like it.' Nick didn't seem overly displeased with the dog, merely ordering him to get in behind. Still displaying his ingratiating grin, Rusty obediently tucked himself behind the big grey horse.

It was piercingly good to ride like this, the two horses ambling along side by side with the ease of long acquaintance. Everything smelled fresh and revitalised; from the branches of a *totara* tree a thrush carolled an ecstatic little song that shrilled its way into Minerva's heart. She took deep breaths of the damp, sweet air as she looked around.

'I think the rain's easing,' she said.

'Yes. See, the sky is lighter over there. You can actually see clouds. It will be fine tomorrow.'

Rusty put up an indignant hare and disappeared, barking furiously, behind a clump of trees. A herd of interested young cattle immediately thundered across the paddock, skittish as lambs, pretending to be afraid.

Minerva's face lit up. 'I've missed this,' she said impulsively. 'It's so beautiful here.'

'The weather didn't give you a dislike of the place?'

She smiled. 'No. I just wished I'd been here longer. I didn't really have a chance to see anything of Spanish Castle...' Her voice trailed away. For a few moments she had forgotten why she had fled over a year ago. Hastily, before he could say anything, she tacked on, 'I couldn't believe my eyes that first day when you solidified out of the mist with Rusty over your saddle. First the smashed signpost, then that. I thought, Oh, hell, here's Igor! No bats, though; only a dog.'

Nick's laugh rang out over the paddock. 'It's a wonder you didn't turn and flee.'

'I suppose I was curious. Why was Rusty riding with you that day? Do you make a habit of carrying him about?'

'No. He'd picked up a gorse prickle in his foot and was limping badly.'

So he remembered that day as clearly as she did.

Nick went on, 'You looked terrified, great dark eyes peering at me from underneath an umbrella.'

'I was a bit alarmed,' she said with dignity. 'More angry, actually, with whoever had smashed the signs.'

He looked straight at her, his hard, handsome face set. 'Alarmed and angry? Was that all? You scared the hell out of me.'

A raging curiosity got the better of common sense. 'Why?'

'Don't you know, Minerva?'

She shook her head. His twisted smile seemed more ironic than normal.

'So blind,' he mocked. 'It must be deliberate.'

Oh, it would be very easy to forget all her resolutions. Ruth's suggestion must have worked some kind of curse during the night, because for a dangerous second Minerva was ready to surrender without asking for anything in return. Her mouth hardened. She didn't dare. If he didn't love her, then all that glittering, potent sexuality was worth very little.

Miraculously, without any intervening drizzle, the rain stopped, allowing a stray sunbeam to penetrate the clouds and find the ground. The air was still so drenched with moisture that it was more like swimming than riding, but the pall of clouds was thinning to the north, shredding into streamers that were already burning up under a hearty sun.

Minerva very much wanted to ask him to clarify his comment, but something held her back. Fear, she thought as the sound of the creek grew louder. If it meant nothing, she'd be shattered.

In spite of her turmoil, happiness, pure and un-nerving, a keen lance of emotion, irradiated her being as surely as the sun brought warmth and light to the countryside. Although she kept her face sternly forward, she knew that Nick was watching her.

It was almost a relief when they reached the top of the rocky face that led to the waterfall. The ancient eruption which had pushed the stream of lava forward had left great boulders scattered at its foot; many had been picked up and broken into fragments to use in the stone walls that separated the paddocks, but there were enough left to make the going a little dangerous.

Nick went ahead, turning frequently to make sure she was coming safely, although on Mixed Biscuits it was practically impossible to make a wrong move. However, catfooted though the mare was, she managed to stumble over a tuft of grass and slid the last few feet down a low bank.

Nick swung around as Minerva and the mare arrived in a little rush. 'Are you all right?' he demanded fiercely, scanning her upturned face with eyes the colour of the rain.

She nodded.

'You've been driving me mad,' he muttered, and bent his head and kissed her, his mouth cold and then hot, tasting of rain and the potent flavour of male.

Without any attempt to protect herself, Minerva went under, caught in the driving heat of his kiss as surely as a butterfly snared by a spider.

It was the horses that recalled them to their sur-roundings. When Demon gave an indignant snort and moved sideways, and Mixed Biscuits tossed her head, their riders broke apart.

Nick's lean hand on the reins let the stallion know who was boss, but his eyes never left Minerva's face. 'We need to talk.'

A tentative happiness exploded within her. 'Yes,' she said.

His teeth showed momentarily white in the darkness of his face. 'But we'll look at the waterfall first,' he said.

Minerva needed time to calm down, to control the turbulence his kiss had aroused: time to remind herself that kisses were cheap. Love cost a lot more, and she wouldn't be content with anything other than his love and his total commitment.

Several minutes later they reached the falls. Rain had expanded a narrow shimmer of silver into a wide, tumultuous veil of water across the sheer face of black volcanic stone, dashing headlong into the flooded pool at the base.

'It's impressive,' Minerva said. 'And very beautiful. I wouldn't have thought we'd had enough rain to do that.'

'It only takes a couple of inches.' He turned Demon towards the steep track through the bush that led up to more paddocks at the top of the bluff. 'Let's go and see what the creek's like up there.'

They didn't speak as the horses walked quietly through the stillness beneath the dark trees and the treeferns. Fantails came fluttering out to greet them, and thrushes and blackbirds found worms that had been flooded from their holes.

The emptiness in Minerva's stomach was apprehension. Absently she touched a mouth made tender by Nick's kiss. She needed to know that he wanted her, not because she was Stella's sister, not even because he desired her and she was suitable; she had to be convinced that he loved with all the fire and passion he was capable of, with everything he was, because that was how she loved him.

Once out of the bush the noise on the waterfall below was overtaken by the roar of the creek. It was still inside its banks, but only just. Water raced towards the bluff in a thick brown foam, taking chunks of the bank with it, tossing twigs and leaves and branches in a headlong rush to the cliff, swirling angrily ever closer to the roots of a sturdy *totara* tree on the edge.

Silver Demon jibbed sideways, but Nick's commanding hand persuaded him to stand still. The mare stood quietly, not seeming to mind the noise or the impetuous tumult of water. Rusty, who had long given up on the hare and rejoined them, sat with his head tilted to one side, alert, intelligent eyes following the islands of froth and grass as they hurtled downstream.

'I suppose,' Nick said, keeping his eyes ahead, 'you terrified me because I took one look at you and knew you were going to make a huge difference to my life, and, quite frankly, it was the last thing I wanted.'

A mounting apprehension cracked Minerva's voice. She swallowed, then muttered, 'I don't understand.'

'I didn't understand, either. I loved Stella; I'd spent a year trying to make some sort of life with her, and another year mourning her and wallowing in guilt. I was off women completely. Then I saw a pale face with a full, kissable mouth, and eyes the colour of a summer midnight, and the bottom fell out of my world.'

'Really?' she said, trying to speak objectively, to tamp down the excitement that roiled through her. 'I don't normally make such an immediate impression. I'm not even pretty.'

'It's been a long time since I've thought of you as anything other than beautiful.' He even sounded as though he meant it.

Scepticism sharpened her voice. 'That's even harder to believe.'

'Why?'

She looked down at the seething water. 'Because you're an intelligent man,' she said roughly, 'and you know damned well that I'm nothing out of the ordinary. I think I'll head back home.'

His hand snaked out to catch the bridle just above the bit, holding Mixed Biscuits steady. 'Is that why you've been so bloody aloof?' he demanded. 'Because you've got some stupid fixation about being plain?'

'I've never had a taste for being second best,' she retorted, anger glinting like stars in her eyes.

A white line had appeared around his mouth. 'Well, by God,' he said dangerously, 'it seems there's only one way I can convince you...'

He was going to kiss her again. She opened her mouth to protest, but a flash of movement behind him brought an urgent cry to her lips. 'Nick—Rusty! No!'

So quickly that she gasped, Nick released the mare and urged Demon after Rusty, who had ventured too close to the creek and was already going down, his first involuntary yip of terror and surprise drowned by the flood.

Setting her teeth, Minerva followed. The ground was boggy and dangerous, but for once luck was with them when they needed it and neither horse stumbled. Minerva shouted, 'Look, there he is!'

Rusty was swimming strongly towards a log that had been swept down in a previous flood and snagged across two rocks in the bed of the stream. Unfortunately this flood was at a higher level and when he struggled up on to the unstable, waterworn timber and tried to shake himself it twisted, dunking him again.

'No,' Minerva groaned.

But Rusty got himself out again, and this time he didn't move.

She opened her mouth to call encouragement.

'Shut up,' Nick said quietly.

'But——'

'The waterfall's only fifty metres downstream. Would you guarantee he'll make it to a bank if he tries to swim back?'

Minerva drew in a sharply painful breath. 'No.'

'If we call him that's what he'll try to do.'

She bit her lip, her eyes fixed on Rusty. The dog was watching them, clearly expecting his master to give him an order, and equally ready to die doing it.

'What can we do?' Minerva asked in a muted voice.

Dismounting, Nick stripped off his riding coat and unlooped the coil of rope he always carried. 'I'm going to get him,' he said calmly.

Minerva's horrified eyes took in the turbulent water, the branches and sticks that hurtled downstream, then moved down to the tumbled rocks and foaming channels where the creek went over the lip. Panic tasting stark on her lips, she said, 'No, Nick, don't go, it's too dangerous.'

'It won't be dangerous at all. I'll tie the rope around myself and loop it around that branch on the *totara*. You can hold it steady and pull us slowly back when I've got Rusty. I'll be perfectly safe.'

His expression told her he was going to do it, with or without her help. She said tonelessly, 'All right.'

Actually, it went as simply as rescue attempts rarely did. At one stage, when it seemed as though Rusty might jump into the water towards his rescuer, Minerva's teeth clamped down on her lip to hold back the hasty words. However, a stern order from Nick kept the dog still.

Waiting for long, helpless moments, Minerva flexed her fingers around the strong rope, her eyes fixed on Nick's tall, strong figure as he waded across the treacherously slippery rocks, then through the channel. It was much deeper than she expected there, up as far as his waist. The next step he took dropped him into water as high as his chest; he staggered, but kept his footing.

'Be careful,' Minerva breathed, watching with painfully widened eyes as he climbed out of the channel and back into shallow water.

He moves so confidently, she thought, trying to convince herself that he'd get back easily. If she tried to wade across the floodwaters she'd probably trip over the stones and end up drowning herself or being swept over the waterfall. But Nick was as cautious and agile as an animal, moving with a lithe, fluid grace that took him closer and closer to the waiting dog.

'He's going to be all right,' she said soothingly to Demon, who was standing a few feet away, ears pricked as he watched. She risked a glance at Mixed Biscuits. The mare was cropping grass. 'Oh, you're very positive. Not worrying a bit, are you?' Minerva said on a half-laugh.

A limb from some long-dead tree came churning down the creek; it wasn't very big but there were no leaves to cushion the impact of the branches. As Minerva choked back a warning shout Nick flung up his arm and half turned away, but even so a sharp twig ripped down his arm, scratching the copper skin. Ignoring it, Nick took the final two steps to the log where Rusty crouched, his eyes fixed on the wet face of his master.

Minerva's teeth clenched on to her lip. She brushed a hand across her eyes as though she could stop the sight of the blood welling in a thin line up Nick's arm and across his chin.

With a firm grip on the dog's collar he set off back.

Minerva eased the loop free and began to move back, holding the line taut, making sure that Nick was kept on his feet all the time.

When he arrived on shore, drenched, blood oozing across his chin, she was waiting with a handkerchief. As she pressed it to the cut she said between her teeth, 'Don't you ever do anything like that again.'

His brows merged over his nose. He looked forbidding and arrogant and angry. 'How will you stop me?'

Rusty shook himself all over them and sneezed several
times.

'I'm going to marry you,' she said, to her complete
astonishment, 'and then I'm going to keep you on a very
short leash.'

The frown smoothed out. Angular features devoid of
any expression, pale eyes gleaming, he stared at her. Then
one eyebrow lifted. 'I don't know what gave you the
idea that I needed a dominatrix,' he said neutrally.

Might as well, she decided with giddy determination,
be hung for a sheep as a lamb. She snorted. 'I don't care
what you need. At the moment it's what I need that I'm
concerned about. And what I need is a real live husband
to——'

'Go on,' he said softly, when her tongue refused to
say the words. 'You've come this far; you might as well
finish it.'

'I don't know what you're thinking,' she wailed.

Slits of silver gleamed behind his thick, curling lashes.
'Nothing venture, nothing win.'

'I hate you,' she said.

'Stop stalling. You want a husband to what?'

'To love,' she shouted, thrusting the handkerchief into
his hands as she whirled around and sprang up into
Mixed Biscuits' saddle. Startled, but obedient as ever,
the mare scrambled away sideways. Submerged beneath
a wave of complete humiliation, Minerva urged her
across the sodden paddock as though all the devils in
hell were in hot pursuit.

Only one was. Clods of earth flicking up from his
heels, Silver Demon came beside her like vengeance itself.
Nick leaned down, caught the bridle in one lean, strong
hand and inexorably brought them to a halt.

'I can,' he said, not even breathing heavily, 'sweep
you on to my saddlebow if you want me to, but then

we'd all of us get very wet, and Mixed Biscuits might well wonder what the hell was going on. Shall we just take it for granted? Would you like to tell me how you feel about me before I wrestle you to the ground and force the words from that wholly delicious mouth?'

She looked up, and what she saw in the darkly intent face gave her courage. 'I love you,' she said baldly.

The freezing fire in his eyes began to heat up but he made no answer, merely stared at her. She was starting to shrivel inside when he said, 'About bloody time!'

'Is that all you can say?'

'It's all I feel like saying, to be quite honest. Do you have any idea of the hoops you've put me through? I've spent untold nights walking the floor and taking cold showers, I've watched you for signs of your feelings until I've longed for blindness——'

'*Do—you—love—me?*'

He drawled, 'Of course I love you. Do you think I'd waste all that anguish and intensity on anything else?'

Minerva looked at him. There wasn't a hint of tenderness in his face; he was watching her with the fierce possessiveness of a primitive man. No gentle lover, Nick Peveril, but she wouldn't have it any other way.

Something unregenerate and proud rose to meet that hungry regard. Half veiled into sultriness, her eyes kindled; the firm discipline that kept her mouth under subjection relaxed to reveal a fervent, willing ardour.

He groaned, and his hand moved from the bridle, reached towards her face. She could have whimpered when she saw him reimpose control. His hand fell to his side.

Unevenly, he said, 'Let's get back to the house.'

They rode side by side all the way back to the homestead. The grey peak that thrust up behind it was still lost in the clouds, but the house shone triumphant in its gardens and trees, foliage glistening with moisture, flowers holding up chalices filled with sweetness. Neither spoke. Minerva felt as Eve must have felt on the first day, so overcome with pleasure and anticipation and wonder that conversation was impossible.

Once inside, the excitement was replaced by shyness. Quickly she stripped off her riding coat and souwester and hung them in the mud-room, then turned to go. He was pulling his T-shirt over his head.

Minerva swallowed. 'I'll get you a robe,' she said, eyes lingering compulsively on the wide expanses of copper skin.

He grinned. 'There's one in the shower.'

She dashed in and found it. When she got back he had only his briefs on. Minerva looked at him, and said helplessly, 'You are so beautiful.'

The amusement died in his face, was replaced by a fierce concentration that turned her heart over. But even as he walked towards her he shivered, and she said, 'Let's go up quickly, before you get chilled. Perhaps you should have a shower here.'

That glittering, feral look faded slightly. 'No, not here,' he said, taking the robe from her and shrugging into it. 'I'll wait until I get to my room. This is no place for me to do what I want to do to you, anyway.'

Desire took her breath away, but she stepped prudently back. Side by side they walked down the passage and when first Ruth, then Brian, came out of the billiard room, he took her hand.

Both pairs of eyes homed in on the movement. Both flicked up to travel first from Minerva's composed face to Nick's.

'We are,' Nick said calmly, 'getting married as soon as possible.'

Pandemonium followed. It kept on following until late that night when, slightly giddy with champagne and full of the delectable food Mrs Borrows had served them for dinner, Minerva shut herself into her room. She was tired and euphoric, but under it all there was a sneaky, unworthy thread of resentment. Nick had played the gratified, assured fiancé perfectly, but she wished she could read the mind and heart beneath that persona he was so adept at projecting.

He said he loved her. Did it mean the same thing to him that it did to her? Was he helpless before that overwhelming, heart-corroding, sense of powerlessness in the hands of fate?

No. She couldn't imagine Nick being so vulnerable.

And neither was she. Not really. Her hand trembled as she took the pearl studs from her ears. If he hadn't said he loved her she'd have left Spanish Castle and gone to the Antarctic, she'd have made a life for herself, but in her heart there would always have been an emptiness that nothing could fill. Nick's place.

But now she would marry him and she would love him, and it would be enough. They were magic together in bed, and she would never worry about his faithfulness. When Nick made a promise he kept it.

So why did her eyes fill with tears, and her throat constrict painfully as she got out of her clothes and into an oversized T-shirt she had bought in St Thomas a year ago?

A knock on the door made her stiffen. Ruth, of course come to talk over the day, to make plans, to crow a little. Hastily wiping the tears away with the back of her hand, Minerva blew her nose before calling out cheerfully, 'Come in.'

But it wasn't Ruth who came in the door. In fact, it wasn't the door that opened. As Minerva pinned a smile on her face she saw a section of the wall slide back, and Nick walk in, his face expressionless.

Minerva's jaw dropped. 'All right,' she said faintly, 'now tell me there's a dungeon.'

'Not exactly a dungeon.' He pushed the wall back into place. 'It's actually a refuge below the stairs. Old Nicholas thought he might need one some time.'

'Any other surprises?'

He was still wearing the clothes he'd put on after he'd showered the chill of the creek away. He looked big and dangerous and competent and not in the least loving.

'No,' he said.

She gave him a cautious glance, not ready for what she realised was going to be a confrontation of sorts. Brightly, she said, 'Tell me about this kidnapping ancestor of yours.'

'Nicholas?' His ironic smile told her that though he understood what she was doing he was prepared to humour her. 'He was young and hot-headed, a yeoman's son in England, and he fell in love with the wife of the lord of the manor. She was five years older than he was, with a small child.'

'So he kidnapped her? Did she love him?'

'Yes, she loved him, but she loved her daughter, too. Family history says that she even loved her husband, in a way.'

'But not the way she loved Nicholas.'

'No, not like that. He thought he'd win her, but by the time they got to New Zealand he realised that he couldn't. When her husband came for her she went back to England with him, and left their son with Nicholas.'

Minerva's brows drew together. 'What was the husband like?' she demanded.

'A decent sort, apparently. He loved her, too. Apparently in his later years Nicholas admitted that in spite of his jealousy he liked the man.'

'I'll bet she didn't want to go. Or perhaps she was a wimp, and preferred the safely comfortable to the wild unknown.'

His shoulders lifted and fell. 'Who knows, now? Can you cope with the wild unknown, Minerva?'

He was asking a lot. It was a test, she thought with an intuition that made her say, 'You must know that I'd follow you naked around the world.'

Something flickered in his eyes. 'Perhaps that's the sort of wife Nicholas wanted. It's a sad story.'

Yes. 'Did he marry again?'

'No,' he said, 'he didn't.'

She nodded. 'What did she look like?'

'Very beautiful. Apparently we get our eyes from her. And that's enough of my disreputable ancestor.' His brows drew together. 'Is that the sort of thing you usually wear at night?'

The T-shirt, the largest one she could find, came to her knees and was old and saggy, ideal for sleeping in. 'Yes,' she said crisply.

'Then it's just as well,' he told her as he went across and locked her door, 'that from now on you won't be wearing any clothes to bed.'

'What is this?' she asked with a crooked smile. 'Are you going to make sure that this wife will sleep with you, Nick?'

'If need be, yes,' he said, breaking her heart into tiny pieces, each shard cutting through her fragile composure, her even more fragile happiness.

She said quietly, 'You don't have to worry. We've already proved that I can't resist you.'

His smile was bitter, unamused. 'Last time neither of us realised what the hell was happening. This time we will.'

His hands on her shoulders were not painful, but there was an inevitability to their grip that warned her. Any protest would be worse than useless. Nick had come determined to conquer.

Already that first divine recklessness was curling through her body, heating as it went, setting fire to her reservations and inhibitions. If only she could see beyond the silver brilliance of his eyes to the man beneath! He was a fiercely sexual lover, and every part of her longed for the oblivion of his arms and his mouth, the fiery possession of his body, yet she wanted more. She wanted—the man, not just the lover. She wanted all of him.

'Minerva?' he said quietly.

He wasn't going to force her. She knew why. It was as though their lovemaking was guided by what had happened before, as though somehow Stella's sad little ghost was pulling the strings.

The thought made her bold, determined not to allow it, to claim her place in his life. They had both loved Stella, but this was their time.

'Before I left last time you said that you'd only marry to have children,' she said. 'Is this just for children, Nick?'

He showed his teeth in a grin that had something of violence in it. 'No, it is not. I didn't know what I was thinking then—I was still confused between what I felt for Stella and what I was trying desperately not to feel for you. Love hadn't worked for me; it seemed that the safest thing I could do was retreat into pragmatism.'

He closed his eyes, then opened them and looked at her with such urgent, defenceless need that her heart stopped in her breast.

'Minerva,' he said huskily, 'I love you, and I want to marry you because if I can't have you as a lover and a friend and a wife I'm going to be lonely until the day I die. And you would never follow me naked, because I would carry you in my arms, and cover you with my clothes.'

That look, open and unshadowed, those starkly vulnerable words, were all she needed.

Before she had time to consider what she was doing, she pulled the T-shirt over her head and guided his hand to her breast. The guarded self-command that kept his features unreadable was subtly transformed into desire, but her heart shook when she realised that the reins of control were still there.

In this, the moment of greatest physical intimacy, he didn't trust her. No, she thought wisely, he didn't trust himself. He was going to take her with him into heaven, and he was going to hold back the essential wildness she sensed within him. Was he still worried about his ability to take her?

She knew now that he really had believed that he was unable to make love, yet it seemed impossible that a man of such blazing sexual charisma could be rendered incapable. Sometime during the last year it had occurred to her that impotence was one way of retreat from an unbearable situation.

Whatever the reason for his continued restraint, she wasn't going to put up with a careful, cautious loving, however much he made her enjoy it.

Suddenly all thought was lost in her sudden, mindless gasp when his thumb moved slowly over the small, pleading aureole in the centre of her breast. Streamers of glittering sensation unfurled through her.

Just before she went under, she vowed that he, too, would surrender to this passion that sprang so miraculously into life at the kiss of glances, the subliminal call of man to woman.

'Yes,' he whispered as she shuddered. 'Tell me what you want, Minerva. Tell me what you want me to do. I don't want to hurt you...'

Now she knew, now she understood! No other woman in his bed would cry foul, would weep in disgust or fear or anger; he would do what she asked him to and no more. Stella was still there with them.

Her jaw set. While his hands worked their magic on her breasts she leaned forward and rested her head against his shirt, breathing in the potent male aroma, the scent of aroused masculinity.

Holding on to her last shred of will-power, she said, smokily, 'I want whatever you do. Touch me any way you want to, do anything at all to me...'

He didn't like that. She heard and felt the indrawn hiss of breath, looked up into eyes as unreadable as polished pewter, and knew that this was the crunch. Not 'do you love me?' That had been simple. Almost from the first he must have known she loved him. But 'do whatever you want to with me'.

Stella's rejection had wounded him in some essentially vulnerable part of his male psyche. Now he had to learn, to understand not just with that cool, clever brain, but deep down in his gut, that in love, in marriage, there were no holds barred. Minerva would not take less.

Staring into his eyes, she saw the mask dissolve and real feeling revealed: the darkness of pain, and an icy fury, because she was forcing something on to him that he didn't want.

Holding her breath, she waited; he had to choose.

'Tell me,' he commanded gutturally. 'I don't want to hurt you.'

'Nothing you could do would hurt me.'

'Nothing?' His anger increased, fed by an unnerving antagonism. 'Damn you,' he whispered in a rough, shaking voice, and kissed her, his mouth compelling hers open to receive the thrust of his tongue, his arms tightening with brutal impact around her.

She should have been frightened, but, although she felt as though she had just won an exhausting, knock-down, drag-out, bare-knuckled fight, the glory of victory pumped through her in an exhilarating flood.

Almost immediately the blind savagery of that first kiss was superseded by another effort at control. Minerva smiled, her lips crushed and sweet with promises, and pressed herself against him, one hand unbuttoning the thin cotton shirt, the other holding him against her.

'I hurt you,' he said harshly.

She laughed. Her mouth stung a little, but one way or another she was going to make him realise that she was not her sister, that his honest passion was not repulsive to her, that she trusted him not to harm her.

'If I bite you,' she said throatily, touching her lips to the hard swell of muscle revealed by her busy hands, 'here,' she bit into the skin, not attempting to hurt, but not holding back either, 'are you going to cry and run away?'

She felt the momentary flinch, felt the sensual flick of her tongue shudder through his body, the sudden tension that followed it.

'No,' he said, the words barely making it through a mouth that was thin and straight, his eyes glittering behind the screen of his lashes, 'I won't cry and run away. Do it again.'

'Only after you do it to me.'

'Do you know what you're asking for?'

She looked up into his face, her own serene and calm and every bit as determined as his. 'Oh, yes,' she said, the words edged with a challenge she made no attempt to hide. 'I know exactly what I want. Do you know what you want?'

Their gazes duelled, neither giving an inch. When he closed his eyes Minerva knew she had won, but any satisfaction died as he picked her up and carried her across to the bed, saying harshly, 'Very well, but on your own head be it. The trouble with knowing what you want is that sometimes you get it, and discover that it really wasn't what you wanted after all.'

'I trust you,' she said, shaken but still valiant. 'All I want is for you to trust yourself, too.'

'Lady,' he said, dropping her into the middle of the bed, 'you don't know what you're asking.'

He went to pull his shirt off but she said, 'No.'

His hands stilled. He looked down at her, and for a fraction of a second she saw a cold weariness that chilled her to her soul.

'Why should you have all the fun? I like undressing you,' she said seriously, and sat up on her heels, her hair streaming down her back. With trembling fingers she pushed his shirt down over his arms and off. He stayed very still, although she could see the faint dampness of sweat sheen his skin. A small, almost smug smile curled her mouth as she started on the fastenings of his trousers.

The iron muscles across his midriff clenched. Leaning forward, Minerva kissed the smooth sleek skin, transforming the kiss into a tiny nip. A soft sound reverberated in the middle of his chest. She smiled, and leaned her cheek against him while she freed him from his clothes. Even though she knew what to expect, she had to force her hands to keep moving, pushing the material over his lean hips, will herself not to show shock or apprehension.

He was all magnificent male, and she cupped him tenderly, bending her head, hair falling like a stream of pale light around them.

'Darling, no, not now,' he said in an anguished voice, and pulled her up against him as he kissed her, putting into the kiss everything he felt, everything he wanted, the full strength of his need.

Somehow they were both down on the bed, his lean, blatantly aroused body poised over hers as he muttered, 'I can't wait—Minerva, stop me——'

'Don't be such a fool,' she said lovingly, wriggling under him, opening, taking him inside her, the silken sheath of her body enclosing him in a clasp as powerful in its female way as the full force of his shaft.

He had been right. She had really had no notion of what she was inviting. But she had been right, too, to throw down that gauntlet. She lifted her hips to accept him as he drove home, and held him in a grip that didn't slacken even when that first impatient thrust almost split her in half.

And then his climax came, strong and fast and fierce, and he called out her name and spilled into her, and still she held him, held him as he collapsed on to her, held him with love and a vital, womanly authority that was entirely new to her.

He went to move but she tightened her arms around him. 'No,' she said into his chest, 'I like this.'

'I hurt you.' He looked down at her with torment in his eyes.

'You did not hurt me. You could never hurt me. You were made to be there, and I was made to take you. I am not Stella, Nick. *I am not Stella.*'

He lifted himself up on to his elbows and said, 'I think I'm beginning to realise that. But you weren't ready, and you didn't come.'

Her eyes gleamed wickedly as she stroked a forefinger along his hip with carefully calculated caution. 'So, we can do something about that, can't we? And now that you've taken me when I wasn't ready, done the absolutely worst thing that can happen, and I haven't shattered to bits, doesn't that prove something?'

He laughed, but somehow the sound had more of a sob in it than any amusement. Lowering his head, he lay with his cheek against her breasts, holding her as gently, as tenderly as he would a child.

'God, I love you,' he said. 'I don't deserve you, Minerva, but I'm bloody glad you're a warrior like the goddess you were named after. Now, about that climax— I seem to remember you find some of the ways and means of getting there very enjoyable...'

Beginning to show her what he meant, he soon found the teaching so very erotic that he was able to finish his ministrations in the most satisfying method of all for both of them, buried deep in her while she cried his name in a soaring paean of ecstasy, her whole being caught up in a world where nothing mattered but the exquisite sensations that were surging through her, each wave tossing her higher and higher up on some unknown shore, until at last she convulsed in his arms, racked by rapture beyond any imagining.

He followed almost immediately, and this time, safe in each other's arms, they slept.

Minerva woke some time in the early hours, and felt his fingers in the long tangle of her hair across his shoulders and chest.

'Mmm?' she said, turning her head into the sound of his heart.

'Go back to sleep.'

But she was instantly awake. 'Why?' she said.

'You must be exhausted.'

She ran an investigatory finger over the hard sheet of muscle across his thigh, smiling with catlike pleasure as it contracted beneath her touch.

'Am I in love with a tease?' he asked.

She said demurely, 'I thought you were only a tease if you refused to come through. I am perfectly willing.'

His chest lifted in a sighing laugh. 'When can we get married?'

'How long does it take?'

'Three days. But don't you want a proper wedding? White dress, ten bridesmaids, three hundred guests?'

'I want you,' she said, making it plain. 'As soon as possible.'

'Ruth will be disappointed.'

'Ruth,' she told him firmly, 'will just have to go without. Anyway, she had that with Stella.'

'Yes.' There was no tension in his voice, nothing but acceptance. After a moment he said, 'I can say her name, think of her now without that awful guilt and pain and anger. Life threw her a forward pass, didn't it?'

'It did. No one should have to go through what she did.'

They were both silent, bidding her goodbye.

'My dearest love,' he said slowly, his voice as uneven as his smile, 'I can't tell you what it means to have you here, safe in my heart at last. I think I fell in love with you the moment I saw you; I certainly knew I wanted to marry you after the first time we made love, but I was still haunted by Stella. I was so angry with her, and so paralysed by guilt, still afraid to look at my emotions in the clear light of day. Then, when you told me what had happened to her, I had to cope with that. I couldn't ask you to marry me without dealing with her memory. I knew that I loved you, but I thought—oh, I thought I wasn't worthy of you, that all the emotions I had had were expended on Stella, and that all I could offer you was second best.'

'So you decided you'd have a nice, sensible marriage with Genevieve Chatswood,' she said on a snap.

He kissed her throat. 'No. There's nothing there but friendship now.'

Minerva's hand slid languorously up his side. She thought he was being a trifle ingenuous; clever Genevieve might have pretended to be content with friendship, but she had almost certainly been heading slowly in another direction entirely. Still, it didn't matter now.

'You didn't write,' Nick said on a steely note. 'Except for that bloody stiff letter saying you weren't having my baby. I threw it in the rubbish, then got it out and hid it in my private papers, because it was all I had of you. You didn't send any messages through Ruth—I was sure I'd queered my pitch well and truly when I made love to you.'

'We both needed time to recover.' She touched his mouth with loving fingers. 'A year seemed enough.'

His chest lifted as he laughed softly. 'An interminable year haunted by eyes the colour of midnight. I was coming to get you, you know.'

'What?' She lifted her head to look into his face. The moon shone in through the uncurtained window, revealing the bold, resolute features. His mouth was curled in the lop-sided smile she loved, but there was an uncompromising determination in his expression that told her he meant what he said.

'Oh, yes,' he said. 'I was going to fly in, plead my case, and if you threw me out I was going to kidnap you. Just like Nicholas.'

'I don't believe that!' But she did.

His smile was narrow and goading. 'But not entirely like Nicholas, because I wouldn't have let you go. You're mine, as much part of me as I am part of you. I couldn't let you leave me now. Fortunately I didn't have to go to such lengths, because Ruth said you were coming back.

So I waited—impatiently. And one look at you—no, I didn't even see you! I knew you were there for some minutes before you actually appeared. I felt you with my skin.'

She said, 'I watched you from behind the palms. You didn't look as though your skin was crawling.'

'Didn't I?'

She remembered then that he had turned and looked around.

He said thoughtfully, 'Actually, it's more of a prickle, an awareness rather than a physical sensation. Not that it matters. From that first glance, that moment our eyes met, I knew that I wasn't going to let you get away this time, so I organised Christmas up here.'

'Organised it?'

'Yes, of course. The next morning, with Ruth. Before you came down to breakfast.'

No wonder Ruth had made assumptions!

'But you've been so bloody elusive,' he said grimly. 'You looked at me as though you hated me. So I was afraid to push my suit. And at the back of my mind there was this fear that I might harm you.'

'Did you hurt Stella?'

'No, but sometimes I wanted to.' His voice was sombre. 'I loved her, but I grew to hate her, as well. And I despised myself for still wanting her when she was so obviously terrified and repelled. Sometimes I'd dream that I was raping her, and I'd wake aroused. It sickened me. *I* sickened me. If only I'd known!'

It sounded as though perhaps her reading of the situation had some element of the truth. Nick's body had simply made it impossible for him to carry out his worst fears. One day she might tell him, but it could wait.

'What could you have done?' she said gently. 'Understanding and sympathy only go so far, Nick. She needed more help than you could give. And for some reason she couldn't ask for it, poor love.'

'So she died,' he said sombrely.

Minerva's throat blocked. She swallowed and said huskily, 'We all made mistakes, but, as Ruth now accepts, at the time we did what we thought was right.'

'Perhaps. Somehow, by some rare kindness of fate, I've got you. Undeservedly, yet you're mine.' He turned his face into the silken spread of her hair across the pillows. 'Kind and loving and warm, with a generosity I'll warm myself at for the rest of my life. I'll make you happy, Minerva, I swear it.'

'I know.' She kissed his throat and his jaw. 'There's just one thing I want to know. Why didn't you tell the coroner about Stella not being able to have children? I know you said it was because that was her business, but that wasn't the real reason, was it?'

She felt his resistance as she spoke, and held her breath.

After several long moments he said heavily, 'She couldn't have children because she'd had chlamydia. She was convinced that it was a punishment for sleeping around. That's why she killed herself. I couldn't risk the possibility of that coming out, darling. It would have humiliated her.'

Yes, he was right. And with the greater insight of her knowledge, Minerva was able to see what had pushed Stella over the edge. Not just that she couldn't have children, but the belief that it was her own actions that had brought it about.

'Poor Stella,' she whispered. 'Poor, poor Stella.'

'I wasn't being entirely noble in keeping it quiet,' he admitted, not attempting to conceal his self-contempt. 'There was a certain amount of self-interest. She told me there was a possibility of in-vitro fertilisation, and I just saw red. It seemed as though she managed very well—she could have children without having to do anything as gross as sleep with me to get them. By then I'd become convinced that she'd married me for money. So I snarled that I wasn't interesting in having children with her. I definitely played my part in pushing her off the edge.'

'You weren't to know.'

He said with bitter intensity, 'If I'd been a little more sympathetic she might have confided in me.'

'I doubt it.' Minerva held her hand against his cheek. 'She never spoke of what had happened to Ruth, even though Ruth told her time and time again that it wasn't her fault. She wouldn't see a therapist. Ruth tried to persuade her to go, but she refused. I don't know that anyone could have helped her.'

He turned his mouth into her palm and kissed it. 'Ruth blames herself,' he said without expression. 'She thinks she should have told me.'

'Do you think she should have?'

He said quietly, 'Possibly. But it's easy to use hindsight, isn't it? We'll never know now.'

'Does it still worry you?'

'I'll regret it until the day I die,' he said evenly, 'but there's nothing I can do about it now. I failed her. I have to live with that. But at the moment, my darling, I can't think beyond the fact that I love you more than I have ever loved anyone, and that you have agreed to marry me, so I'm the happiest man on this earth tonight.'

She kissed him, and he kissed her back, and then asked, 'How did you know I was afraid that I'd hurt you?'

'I could see you were determined to be in control. It didn't need much insight to realise why.'

'Stella's terror bypassed the logical part of my brain and homed in on my ego and my libido. That's where men are most vulnerable. I knew it was irrational, but I couldn't bear to hurt you.'

Lovingly, she kissed his chin. 'Now you know you can't. I can take anything you dish out and give it back to you.'

He stretched, and laughed, and pulled her close. Instantly she felt the return of that honeyed flood of desire; felt too the resurgence of his masculinity against her.

'I love you,' he said, stroking down the length of her body as though she was so rare and precious that he hardly dared touch her. 'I love you with everything I am, everything I have to offer. I'll love you until the day I die.'

It had taken, she thought, just before she surrendered to passion, a long, heartbreaking journey for them to reach their Spanish Castle, the longed-for, rarely achieved goal of all their dreams. But they were there now, and the future lay like some smiling plain before them, rich, and fertile and full of promise.

Fifty red-blooded, white-hot, true-blue hunks
from every State in the Union!

Look for MEN MADE IN AMERICA! Written by some
of our most popular authors, these stories feature some
of the strongest, sexiest men, each from a different state
in the union!

Two titles available every month at your favorite
retail outlet.

In January, look for:

WITHIN REACH by Marilyn Pappano (New Mexico)
IN GOOD FAITH by Judith McWilliams (New York)

In February, look for:

THE SECURITY MAN by Dixie Browning
(North Carolina)
A CLASS ACT by Kathleen Eagle
(North Dakota)

You won't be able to resist MEN MADE IN AMERICA!

HARLEQUIN®

PRESENTS Plus

It wasn't the best start to a working relationship: Debra's private detective sister had asked her to spy on Marsh Graham—Debra's new boss! But if Debra began by believing Marsh had suspicious motives, she soon realized that, when it came to her, Marsh had desires of a more personal kind....

Was Denzil Black moving from woman to woman, seducing them, then leaving them drained and helpless? Clare thought of Denzil as a vampire lover...so when she realized that she was next on his list of conquests, she resolved that *Denzil* would learn what it was to be a victim of love!

In Presents Plus, there's more to love....

Watch for:

A Matter of Trust by Penny Jordan
Harlequin Presents Plus #1719

and

Vampire Lover by Charlotte Lamb
Harlequin Presents Plus #1720

Harlequin Presents Plus
The best has just gotten better!

Available in February, wherever Harlequin books are sold.

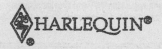

HARLEQUIN®

Don't miss these Harlequin favorites by some of our most
distinguished authors!
And now, you can receive a discount by ordering two or more titles!

HT#25577	WILD LIKE THE WIND by Janice Kaiser	$2.99	☐
HT#25589	THE RETURN OF CAINE O'HALLORAN by JoAnn Ross	$2.99	☐
HP#11626	THE SEDUCTION STAKES by Lindsay Armstrong	$2.99	☐
HP#11647	GIVE A MAN A BAD NAME by Roberta Leigh	$2.99	☐
HR#03293	THE MAN WHO CAME FOR CHRISTMAS by Bethany Campbell	$2.89	☐
HR#03308	RELATIVE VALUES by Jessica Steele	$2.89	☐
SR#70589	CANDY KISSES by Muriel Jensen	$3.50	☐
SR#70598	WEDDING INVITATION by Marisa Carroll	$3.50 U.S. $3.99 CAN.	☐ ☐
HI#22230	CACHE POOR by Margaret St. George	$2.99	☐
HAR#16515	NO ROOM AT THE INN by Linda Randall Wisdom	$3.50	☐
HAR#16520	THE ADVENTURESS by M.J. Rodgers	$3.50	☐
HS#28795	PIECES OF SKY by Marianne Willman	$3.99	☐
HS#28824	A WARRIOR'S WAY by Margaret Moore	$3.99 U.S. $4.50 CAN.	☐ ☐

(limited quantities available on certain titles)

	AMOUNT	$
DEDUCT:	**10% DISCOUNT FOR 2+ BOOKS**	$
ADD:	**POSTAGE & HANDLING**	$
	($1.00 for one book, 50¢ for each additional)	
	APPLICABLE TAXES*	$_____
	TOTAL PAYABLE	$_____
	(check or money order—please do not send cash)	

To order, complete this form and send it, along with a check or money order for the
total above, payable to Harlequin Books, to: **In the U.S.:** 3010 Walden Avenue,
P.O. Box 9047, Buffalo, NY 14269-9047; **In Canada:** P.O. Box 613, Fort Erie, Ontario,
L2A 5X3.

Name: _____

Address: _____ City: _____

State/Prov.: _____ Zip/Postal Code: _____

*New York residents remit applicable sales taxes.
 Canadian residents remit applicable GST and provincial taxes.

HBACK-JM2